BAD RECEPTION

SHANNEN WRIGHT

SNOW LEOPARD PUBLISHING

Bad Reception
Copyright © 2016 Shannen Wright

For information contact :
Snow Leopard Publishing
http://www.snowleopardpublishing.com
email: info@snowleopardpublishing.com

ISBN: 978-1-94436123-5 (paperback)
      978-1-94436124-2(hardcover)
      978-1-94436125-9(ebook)

LCCN: 2016940184

Cover Design by J Asheley Brown Designs

First Edition: May 2016

10 9 8 7 6 5 4 3 2 1

This book goes out to anyone and everyone who helped me over the past year. Thank you, Daniel, the love of my life, for your unwavering support throughout the last year. Thank you for your help, John, with my novice writer questions! And thank you to everyone in the "Switchblade" group for your help and support too.

1

The train rumbled across the barren strip of wasteland, though the young brunette woman had no idea where in the arid country she was. It was late. She was tired, hungry, and her child clung to her breast with a low whine in his chest, hunger the only thing in his belly. Unlike the other Mothers on the overcrowded train who were publicly breast-feeding, his Mother had no milk for him. The girl was far too embarrassed, anyway. The women eyed her with disdain; some more than others, so she remained quiet and curled in her corner, silently begging for some reprieve from the insistent crying of her beloved child.

She stood apart from the other dark-skinned native Indian travellers. Her pale skin shone white enough to look ill. Her delicate build, while perhaps being malnourished, did not look starved, but her child's body did. His tiny fists beat and pawed at her clothing, an uncomfortable reminder that he had not fed in far too long.

"Come Michael. Please baby, hush hush." She whispered at him with a mysterious accent. British, or perhaps Scottish, but with a lilting trace of something else, something further North. Norway? No, Swedish. Just the tiniest hint of it in her voice. She spoke quietly, hiding; evidently afraid if she spoke too loudly something terrible would happen.

She pursed her lips in thought and glanced toward the window again. Darkness slowly spread across the amber sky. Already she could see the ghost dust of stars. Not as many as would be seen in the outskirts the carriage would soon pass, but enough to make her smile in recollection of a rather old memory. She missed home, of that there could be no doubt but turning back could no longer be considered an option.

No luxury cruise, this; the boxcar reeked of squalor. She was blessed with the exceptional good fortune to find a seat on an over-turned bucket. This passenger carriage housed nearly thirty huddled passengers and their clinging children; still it was the best of the available options at the time. Above them, rickety makeshift shelves with dirty beds housed about ten more people lying in the tightly packed space.

The young woman's eyes felt drawn toward one passenger in par-ticular; a young man alone, neatly groomed and well dressed, who stood out in shocking contrast to the rest of the passengers, women and children all. He sat with a holdall and a metal flask filled with something hot and savoury. She could smell it from where she sat. Her stomach growled.

What little colour remaining in her cheeks drained as he caught her looking; yet he smiled pleasantly before returning his attention to the floor at his feet. The other women all huddled together, appar-ently pulling themselves communally away from the lone man. The young girl could hardly blame them. It could be dangerous out here, in this area of India, especially for unaccompanied women.

Summoning her courage, she stood up, small and huddled, and picked her way toward him. Her small body took that space separat-ing him and the rest of the passengers. Her previous space rapidly vanished under a shapeless woman and her four year old, who settled down and draped across her knee.

"You seem to have found the wrong carriage." Kana whispered

to him, still holding her wriggling child tightly. She glanced apologetically at the young man, who immediately furrowed his brows as he reached for his bag.

"Wait. Please?" Her hand reached for his wrist, grabbing the fabric of his warm jacket with a force more rough that she intended, and more panic in her voice that she had hoped. She could not let him leave yet. "You're like me, right? A tourist?"

"Yeah, all the way from New York." The man's Brooklyn accent was unmistakable. The knowledge immediately drew a nervous smile from her. Although a friendly man, she noticed he recoiled from her icy touch. "My name's Theodore, Theodore Schmidt, but everyone just calls me Theo. I'm out here for a year outta school. College, y'know."

She gave another smile and nodded. He seemed safe, but there was no telling with some people; he could just as easily have a gun in his bag as not. "I'm Kana. I'm from Scotland originally. Nice to meet you."

"Pleasure, miss. You been in India long?"

"No, a few days at best. You?"

The American shook his head. " 'Bout a week. Heading to Kanyakumari. My idiot friend said it'd be a fun train ride." he waved his hand, bringing a strained giggle from the Brit. "Whoop dee do."

Kana nodded, shuffled her jean-clad legs into a tight cross-legged position, the denim taut but worn and dusty. She shifted her child up. The American's eyes lingered on the boy.

"Excuse me for asking, but. how old are you, miss?"

Kana inwardly sighed. Every time. In less developed countries, usually people questioned why she was travelling without a man; in more developed countries, they questioned how old she was, looking too young to be carrying a child.

"Old enough to have a one and a half year old, legally." The annoyed bite to her voice brought shock to his face. "Sorry. I'm twenty-five, I just look young." A practised lie, but she gave a contrite look and cast her gaze downwards. So much for playing it coy.

"Yeah, I could see that." Theodore nodded. "You look young for your age, many girls do. It's all that make up most wear. It's unnatural."

"Oh, definitely." Kana's eyes rolled in the darkness, unseen. Or so she thought. Theodore's chuckle brought her blue gaze back to his. Brown, she noted.

"What?"

"You just rolled your eyes at me."

She blinked, embarrassed, and then: "What's in your flask?"

"Soup. It's just lentil though, nothing fancy." He shrugged. "Why, you hungry?"

"Starving." she admitted, still eyeing the flask. "But not for me, for Michael. We were in a rush today. I forgot to bring him something, and the wee guy is starving." As if on cue, the tiny bundle turned from his Mother's chest to peer with equally blue eyes at Theodore. The American hesitated, winced, and pushed the flask at Kana. Without hesitation, she grabbed it whip-quick, before the stranger could change his mind. Pouring a little into the attached cup, she swirled it slowly, blowing on it to cool the scalding liquid. The sweet smell of the lentils permeated the acrid scent of body odour in the train carriage.

"Aren't you scared out here on your own, just you and the kid?"

"Nah." Kana shook her head, still blowing and flexed her left index finger. On it sat a soft blue sapphire, almost black in colour. It looked like a wedding band, but with no engagement ring beneath it.

"You're married?" The disappointment dripped from his words. Kana barely hid the mirth from her face as she shifted her child, tilting slowly tilt the soup into his mouth. His pink lips moved and twisted into a smile, eager for more.

"No, not married," Kana's voice brimmed with amusement, her gaze still trained upon Michael. "Just an illusion. It makes things easier." She grinned at Theodore. "It fooled you, didn't it?"

"Clever. You seem pretty smart. Aside from the whole forgetting to feed your kid thing."

Kana's focus narrowed into a glare. The wild instinctive urge to launch herself at him almost pulled her to her feet.

"Oh, ay, no need for that look. I was just" he stammered, shocked by her sudden aggression. Hey, y'know what, never mind," and he reached for the flask.

"You have no idea what I've been through for Michael," Kana hissed, twisting to keep the flask with her child."I'm really grateful for the soup for him, thank you so much. But please keep comments like that to yourself." She tried keeping her tone polite. It was hard. Michael, of course, gave not one damn for the nattering grown-ups; his focus was on swallowing the proffered soup. Guilt panged in Kana's own empty stomach. How long had she let him do without? His hands pulled at the cup, trying to guzzle faster, but Kana held it still. With no prospects for more food in the immediate future, this would have to satiate him.

"I'm sorry." His shoulders slumped, allowing the child to feed. "Look, forget I mentioned it. Sometimes I feel clever. It's meant to be funny, but my sense of humour is off. Sometimes t doesn't always come off that way."

An uneasy silence settled over the pair. The rattling of the train and clatter of the rails rocked the pair together but Theo sighed, pulled off his jacket and slung it over Kana's rail thin shoulders. She looked up and frowned.

"What's that for?"

"You gotta be freezing. I can feel your cold body through the jacket. Keep it on till you get off the train, huh?" Kana's smile returned with intensity. The garment wouldn't help in the slightest, but the gesture was deeply appreciated. She pulled it tighter, and said a brief thank you. Michael finished the soup and gave a tiny gurgle of a burp. Kana giggled, and readjusted his weight on her lap. Almost instantly, he settled off into sleep. She rummaged through her bag, pulling out a wet wipe.

"You had time to pack wet wipes but not food?"

Kana clicked her tongue against the roof of her mouth and dabbed Michael's mouth. His hand clung against her t-shirt, tugging it down by a fraction. Theodore's eyes bee-lined toward the slightly exposed cleavage. Noticing, Kana pulled the jacket around both girl and the babe.

" I had a lot of things on my mind and not much in the house." Guilt washed her insides. With the baby fed, the burden of civility in this miserable environment had taken on more weight; but for the sake of future meals for Michael, she wanted Theo to stay amicable.

And yet, she felt driven to bite back, "If raising a baby was easy, maybe they'd let men do it."

"Hey wow, jeez.," his brown eyes widened. "Sexist much, lady?"

"Sorry." she shook her head, as irritated with herself now as she'd been with him barely a moment ago. "Sore subject. And these accommodations don't do much for my temper. It's not your fault."

"I understand." he looked away and fell silent. After a moment, he looked back and offered, "I used to babysit my brother a lot though, he was a handful."

"Most children are." She managed a smile, then turned her full attention to Michael once again. Cute or no, she did admit Theo was a little bit funny, and generous with his food. She was annoyed with herself, now; was that the kind of person she would become, out here? Again that awkward silence descended on them like a musty blanket.

Okay, maybe he'd given her a loan of his jacket too. With a quiet sigh, she turned back to him.

"Why India?" Small talk. They were back to small talk.

 In return, Theo gave a small shrug and tugged the flask back towards him, clicking it back together. "Well, I'll tell ya, it was either here or China, right? And I'm not really a big fan of the food there. I thought there'd be better curry here. I like spice, know what I'm sayin'?"

"Isn't that kind of a strange thing to base your choice on, just the food?" Kana quirked a brow.

"Is it?" Another shrug. "What about you? Why did you come all the way out here? I mean, is that a good idea to vacation out here with a little kid?"

Kana nodded in agreement. She reached up to brush a strand of downy blonde hair from Michael's eyes. Had it been her call, she never would have put them on a train at all. They would have been at home from the beginning.

Why tell this man the real reason she and Michael had stepped onto a train in the middle of nowhere? She considered, mulling over the lengthy explanation required. The train ride would take five or six hours, and sleeping was the only other option to pass the time. Kana could not sleep, but Michael would.

The clucking of chickens from makeshift rooms echoed through-out the carriage.

"I'm not on holiday," she admitted with a snort of laughter. "I'm running away from home."

It took a few seconds for the American to react, but his eyebrows knotted together, mouth parting. "Seriously? You're running away from home, and you ran all the way to China? Are you, crazy?"

Kana heard panic in his voice, and felt relief wash over her. Theo clearly felt sympathy and worry; maybe not quite the threat she had imagined. In fact, she had already earned clothing and food from him. She had an inkling that if she asked for money he would share his without a fuss.

"It's a matter of life and death." She simply offered. "I did some-thing stupid and dangerous, and I had to leave, for my sake and theirs."

"Theirs? Whose?"

"My family. "

The train gave another heavy lurch and Michael shifted in his sleep. Theo eyed him warily. He opened his mouth to speak but Kana cut him off.

"It isn't about Michael, though he was a result of doing some-thing stupid. Figuratively and literally." Another snort of dry laugh-ter.

"What?" Theo asked warily, but his curiosity was growing, she could see it in his eyes and the way he leaned towards her.

Kana debated. Could she trust him? Complete strangers, having barely met, did not reveal themselves to one another. Not to mention the danger if Theo turned out to be more than he admitted to.

"It's a really long story. Are you sure you want to hear it?" She pushed for time.

Theo pointed around him and out the tiny, half-obscured win-dow. They had left civilization and now the train chugged along open countryside of India. "What else are we gonna do, uh? So maybe you're a whackaloon, who cares. Tell me a story."

A compromise struck her. "Fine, but you must give me the rest of your soup for Michael."

He nodded his assent.

  Perhaps talking would help her solidify things in her mind, and rationalise what to do. Besides, if he reacted badly, she could always kill him.

  Reaching out and pulling the canteen back to herself, Kana shifted her weight towards the wall, effectively making herself comfortable. She twisted the cap a little, sniffed the contents and brought the mixture to her lips as if to drink the concoction, before wrinkling her nose and quickly replacing the cap. She lifted her hand to cover her mouth, and hide the nausea the smell brought. Maybe she'd try some later.

  "It started when I was nineteen." She recalled the facts. "You see, I met some monsters"

2

"When I was just a little girl, no older than six or seven, my mum used to tell me stories before bedtime.

My favourite story was about the cursed monster.

She used to tell me about a scary monster who ran around being mean and bad and terrible; scaring all the people in village with his bad, terrifying deeds. So, this good witch put a curse on him and sentenced him to live forever, losing those he loved just like the innocent families had.

The witch said, "Because of what you've done, because you've hurt so many people and ripped many families apart you will suffer the pain of all these families and suffer just as much as them."

I used to cheer at that bit, thinking the monster deserved it.

And then I got a little older, and thought about how the monster must be in so much pain, must be suffering awfully, must surely have learned his lesson by now?

So, I made up my own stories after dad left.

9

I imagined how sometimes the monster under my bed would get tired of being scary and cry himself to sleep sometimes. He would get lonely or sad or scared too, and he wouldn't want to be a monster anymore. So, he stopped.

But his fellow monsters laughed at him and made him feel worse.

Then he ran away.

But it would be okay because the one monster that was cursed is still around, hiding in plain sight, trying to make the best of a bad deal, trying to make himself happy and trying to make a friend.

The Original Monster had made a little house out in the city where he could gather other monsters who were tired of being monsters and he could make a family for himself. The monster from under my bed could stay with him and be safe.

When I got older, life became more complicated. I didn't have time for stories anymore. The Original Monster was forgotten. I experienced life. I learned life wasn't as clear cut as monsters and heroes.

And then, when I was nineteen years old, I met the Original monster and I ended up going home with her"

"I don't know why you work so hard to ruin everything I plan for you." Her mother's disappointed sigh from the front seat of the small car reached Kana, who slumped lower in the back seat. It was audible even over the mechanical wheezing of the old family car. A sturdy and reliable old machine, it had served them reasonably well for the past five years, despite a few complaints.

"Yeah, Kana." The surly tone of her younger sister intoned from the front seat, the place only the chosen child sat. "It would have literally took you five minutes to put your things away. I put my clothes away the second I was told."

Kana closed her eyes and turned her head, focusing on the world outside the car. The dim light cast from the sleepy lampposts cast pale echoes of itself across the wet tarmac. She stifled a yawn. It was dawn. Some of the lights faded away to nothing; beginning to rest now as the world woke from sleep.

"I do so much for you. Why don't you ever appreciate it?"

"Yeah, Kana," her sister chimed in. "Mum works hard. You could have gone to college or something by now, instead of sponging off her all the time."

Kana bit her tongue for now. No. Not today. Not now. She took in a deep breath. Through the window red brick houses rolled past, green hedges creating a viridian blur. "I don't know why, Mother." She ignored her sister.

"I had planned so much. You were going to enjoy it -- the party, the entertainment, the food. Well, you're not getting that now." Her tone switched from gruff to sweet, "Karen, is it this turn off or the next one?"

"Next one, Mummy."

Kana bit back harsh words. *Do not let her get to you.* She curled her fingernails into her palm, hoping the pain would distract her mind from her mother's persistent criticisms or her sister's cheerleading from the front. She need not have wasted the effort; the car rattled over a hole in the road. Kana yelped as she bounced, a jolt shooting through her leg. She lifted her tracksuit bottoms to examine it, but there was nothing visible. It throbbed like hell though.

"It's your own damn fault, Kana," her mother sniped, turning the wheel, no hint of sympathy to be found. Kana found instead, an overbearing violent urge to slam her mother's head into the steering wheel. She resisted somehow, whining louder at the pain in her leg every time a bump jerked it.

"Of course it is." She finally bit back, hissing through the pain. Her eyes squeezed shut to bear it. "It's my fault I fell down the freaking stairs, it's my fault you left the freaking pile of clean washing on the stairs, and it's my fault we're rushing to the emergency room at seven in the morning on my freaking birthday."

The look Kana caught by way of the rear view mirror demanded she shut up but Kana persisted, her anger now piqued.

"Honestly, Kana, I don't know why you do this to me."

"Do this to you? Right, this is about you. And a delightful bone fracture is more fun than spending the morning with the two of you." Kana retorted, her voice loaded with sarcasm. She wanted to try her mother's patience as equally as her own had been tried. She watched her mother's scowl in the rear view mirror.

"Shut up, Kana." Karen hissed. "That attitude is probably why you don't have a boyfriend. All just because you can't do as your told.

You have two years on me, isn't that time enough to do something with your life --"

"Thank you Karen, it's alright. She's just being ungrateful. I'm used to having an ungrateful daughter. Not you though, Dear."

"Course I am. That's the only reason I exist isn't it? Purely to spite you two."

"Sometimes I wonder, Kana." Their mother sighed and shook her head.

Kana silenced herself and sank further down the scratched vinyl car seat, her arms folding. Her back pressed into the foam. A sign whizzed past outside, alerting them the hospital stood only two more kilometres ahead. Another bump in the road wiped the smile from Kana's face. She let out another yelp as the motion lifted her leg and dropped it back to the seat with force.

"Kana. Must you make so much noise?"

The injured girl seethed. Her jaw clenched with barely concealed frustration. "Oh don't mind me. I'll just sit quietly while my mother's reckless driving rips my bloody leg in half."

"Stop being so melodramatic. You've probably only sprained it. If you'd broken it, you would know all about it."

"I did, and I do."

"Kana." Her mother's voice rose as she jerked the wheel hard to take another sharp bend at high speed. Kana ground her teeth together, her face paling as she fought back a scream, her body tilting into the side of the car. "Will you shut the hell up? I have to decide which turn-off to make."

"No doubt it'll be the one with the biggest potholes. My mother, Colin freaking McCrae" Kana grumbled under her breath. Karol did not hear it, finally turning the ancient Volvo into the car park.

All three shared the same dark-brown, wavy hair that curled at the tips. Karol and Karen wore theirs with a ponytail, while Kana preferred hers loose and free, sprawling down her back. It jostled up and down in the car with every speed bump or crack in the road. Kana had a permanent look of unrelenting boredom glued to her face, while her mother, twenty years her senior, had exasperation etched into hers. The daughters shared the same button nose, the same high cheekbones, and the same bright blue eyes.

The sticky wet noises of the tires rolling across the tarmac stopped. The car finally parked at the emergency bay. Meticulous parking on her mother's part; both car and line were perpendicular. Not a single wheel touched the paint of the bay's markings. Kana's arms slowly folded around each other. The realisation that this was not going to be the nineteenth birthday she had hoped for settled over her like a sodden blanket.

Today might have been easier if her perfect sister hadn't come home for the holidays and just stayed at her pompous university. Kana sulked. Since she received no sympathy from anyone else, she might as well feel sorry for herself.

Karol had left the car, brushed both handsss down her neat business suit and now glared at her daughter through the window of her door. Kana lazily unfolded her arms and rolled down the window.

"Welcome to McDonald's," she said, not missing a beat. "Would you like fries with that?" Her grin was wide.

"Move. Your. Backside. Kana."

"Honestly Kana, grow up." Her sister scolded, climbing out of the passenger side.

Again Kana's arms folded. She didn't move.

"Oh, right," She feigned surprise. "And I suppose you expect me to walk all the way into reception on a broken leg? Do you not think a wheelchair might be in order?"

"Kana, are you fucking five? Get out of the car."

"Shan't."

"Kana, so help me --"

"I hope you're not planning on making a scene, Mothe --"

"The only person making a scene right now is you. Now get out of the fucking car."

Kana hated her mother's lack of patience. Karen covered her forehead with her palm and glanced at the ground, her face flushing red. Finally relenting, Kana slowly made her way out of the car. She exaggerated the motions, limping excessively, but there was no faking the pained expression on her face. Once out of the car, she leaned on her good leg, and caught her breath. Nearby several smokers outside the hospital entrance looked stunned and amused. Clearly they heard every word.

"I'd be quicker fucking crawling. You can't seriously expect me to walk all the way up to the hospital on a broken leg." Kana's eyebrows rose, her teeth clenching as her cheeks paled. Karol checked the time on her blackberry.

"What have I said about language?" Karol snarled, grabbing her daughter's hand and drug her toward the doors. Somehow, perhaps because she knew that protesting would only dial her mother's shouting up to eleven, Kana managed to keep her noises of complaint to a minimum. Her breathing, however, grew laboured.

Karen trailed behind them at a distance.

Once inside, things grew somewhat easier; Kana used the walls for support and eased her way gently along it toward the reception. A few outpatients stared and Karol clicked her tongue.

"Karen, go find a seat, will you, Sweety?"

"Yes, Mum." The seventeen year old hunted down a group of chairs amidst the packed waiting room.

A few steps into the building, Kana's balance faltered on the polished floor. Her good foot slid, causing the other to hit the ground too sharply, and she screamed. All eyes swivelled to face them. The added attention only made Karol more irate; her cheeks flushed. In pain, Kana tuned her out, blue eyes hazing over as she tried to focus on the problem at hand. Or foot.

Kana blinked back tears, then shot the gawkers a venomous look, until they relented and broke eye contact. Then she hobbled toward the reception desk and favoured the receptionist with her best effort at a smile, trying to push away her own frustration. The receptionist, for her part, seemed less than enthusiastic about anything at all.

"Kana Ingrid Lindqvist," Kana introduced herself stiffly, leaning on the desk for support. "I think I've broken my leg."

"Sprained it," intoned a feminine voice from behind her.

"Broke it, sprained it, either way it's fucked."

"Kana." Her mother hissed yet again. "Watch your language."

Kana ignored it, watching the receptionist expectantly.

"Please take a seat," the receptionist droned, "your name will be called when the doctor is ready to examine you." The lady remained disinterested as she passed a sheet of paper to her mother to complete. Kana slowly shuffled to a vacant seat by her sister. Karol followed, keeping a tight grip on her purse. Then only the frantic scribble of pen scratching upon paper was heard.

The heavy silence of the waiting room bore down. People shifted around in their seats, punctuated only by a smattering of coughing. The furtive glances of the other patients fell between the chairs. All scrutinised each other, searching for ailments. Kana could almost hear the complaints already: *You're not ill enough to go before me.* The silent judgement of those who being kept waiting.

"I hope this doesn't take too long." Karol griped, opening her bag and checking her Black Berry upon finishing the medical form.

"It shouldn't. Viola from my English elective is one of my best friends, and she has been telling me that the reforms in the NHS mean things should be totally easier."

"Oh, good. I have a meeting soon anyway."

Kana scowled. She didn't care for her mother's meetings but she knew how important they could be. Her sister, on the other hand, had no reason to be such a suck up. With so many things going for her, Karen was doing more than rubbing salt on an open wound.

She sat in silence, pensive while her mother and sister gossiped away.

While she appreciated that her mother had called in many favours for her birthday, she had personally asked for none of them.

Nineteen. The number made Kana cringe. A proper adult now by all standards, inwardly she still felt like a child. By all rights, she should have been working, or in college, or doing something with her life. Instead, she found herself a mediocre young woman with a mediocre life and a broken leg. She clicked her tongue as she thought about how her mother would invariably press the issue soon.

In fact, Karol must have read her mind because, after a few beeps on her phone, she nudged her daughter, wakening her from her daydream.

"Say, Kana, you know how I work in Human Resources at the company." She gloated. To what end Kana hardly cared but it chilled her core to consider it, so she gave nothing more than a nod of acknowledgement.

"We're looking for Admin staff -- you'd be great in Administration. Computers, you like computers, right? Typing, you'd have to make coffee too, and so on."

"Mum, I don't want to work in Admin."

"Mum, Kana wouldn't do well there. She'd have to clean up after herself." Karen retorted.

"Oh, don't be ridiculous.. You'll be fine.Mr Benson would hire you in a heartbeat. You would have to dress nice, mind. None of your ridiculous outfits. Pencil skirts, not jeans and shirts, not t-shirts. You can't be cheeky to him like you are to me."

Kana zoned out again. Great, stuck in a job with her mother. She fought an urge to run out of the hospital. Her leg did a good deal to help her stay sitting.

"Miss Kana Lindqvist?"

A soft male voice echoed into the room and Kana breathed a quiet sigh of relief. It wasn't quite the rescue she hoped for, but it would provide temporary relief.

"Hurry up, Kana. I'll wait for you here." Her mother waved fondly after her and punched a number into her Blackberry, not looking up from her phone.

***

A few hours later, Kana strained up over the lip of a table in the hospital cafe trying to sip an overpowering milkshake. The strong painkillers the Doctor had prescribed had lulled her into a happy daze, and occasionally she had to reach up and wipe the drool from the side of her mouth.

The chemical smell of artificial strawberry flavour seeped into every corner of the room. With the aid of her mother, she managed to suck the straw between her teeth, though maintaining its position took some effort. The artificially sweetened drink thickly coated her throat, frothing in her mouth. Swallowing it was another adventure. One foot was wrapped around the stirrup of her wheelchair, the other rested on a footrest and was encased in a bulky white cast. Her eyes never left it.

Beside Kana, her sister sat with the remains of a yellow concoction, once a banana milk shake. She had finished hers.

"Perhaps we can colour it in pink?" Karol suggested with an innocent smile. Kana wasn't sure if she referred to the wheelchair or the cast.

"I told you it was broken."

"Shut up, Kana. I said it was broken, you just jumped on the sympathy bandwagon."

Kana felt nauseous, but she let her sister have the moment.

The twinkling ring-tone from Karol's phone silenced them both. Karol plucked it from the table and squinted at it.

"I'm due at a meeting at three." She explained to Kana. "It's important. Plus I have to take Karen back to the campus dorms. I had to call in favours for your birthday and because of this little incident," She pointed to Kana's new cast. "I have to do this to make it up to people after cancelling."

"So you're running me home quickly?"

"No, I'm sorry, darling. I don't have time. Here." She slipped a ten pound note onto the counter. "Taxi, bus, just don't be too late. It can't be helped. I promise I'll buy takeaway for tea."

"Wow, Mum. That's so generous of you. I mean, she's gonna get so much from her birthday. Just make her take the taxi fare from that."

"No, no." Karol insisted. "I think she left it in the house. Talk to you later, Kana. Be good."

Karol slipped away, still tapping at the buttons on her phone, Karen at her heel like a good little puppy.

Kana's face fell. Money or no, the fact that Karol had left her to her own devices immediately after such a traumatic event made her fists clench.

Nothing could be done about it. Karol had flown from the hospital faster than the drugged and half-insensate girl could protest.

She ground her teeth together, fighting the dampness at her eyes. Screw it. If she got stabbed or murdered or whatever on the way home, it would serve her mother and sister right.

Grasping the wheels of the chair, Kana acclimated herself to pushing her way across the cafe.

"Right." She told herself. "I can do this."

She was pretty certain she couldn't do this.

If she reached the taxi rank outside she could get home quite easily. It would only take ten minutes if they took the back road. The cafe now stretched away deserted; no-one could help her if she even summoned the courage to ask, but that also meant at least that no-one would laugh at her if she fell.

Another few pushes, slowly growing used to the turning arc of the wheels, and Kana finally reached the door, lost for ideas. Inevitably, she would have to climb out of the chair to push open the door. She groaned in exasperation.

Alone and unaided, the girl slowly worked her way up into a frustrated fury. She shrieked her frustration out at the door and pulled out her mobile:

For fuck's sake mother,
I can't even get the fucking door open.
How do you expect me to get home if I can't open a door?

Her typing was frenzied. She'd rather have shouted those words than text them. Instantly, a message returned, making her phone ding:

Watch Ur language Kana.

There came no further replies, but Kana found she no longer cared. Rising to her feet, using her body weight as a counter balance, the door finally gave way. She inched through. Outside, the rest of the hospital seemed to be going on as normal until a high pitched siren echoed throughout the cafeteria. Blue eyes glanced back.

What the hell?

It was a hell of a loud siren. Was someone coding down the hall, or had she just set off the fire alarm? Her heart skipped a beat as she wondered. She peered around but could not find a fire exit sign on the door.

Her fears subsided when a flock of nurses flew past along with a security guard. Though desperately curious, Kana lacked the means to follow.

With a sigh of resignation, she turned to pull the wheelchair through. She wobbled precariously, and every time her balance landed on the cast it brought pain rushing up her leg even through the warm fog of the painkillers. She winced.

She had almost pulled the wheelchair through when a mighty thump knocked her sideways. Kana's eyes widened as someone -- or something -- flew into her with enough force to knock her sprawling to the ground. Time seemed to slow down, and her free hand grabbed the nearest thing to prevent her fall: a hooded jumper. She pulled the someone down with her.

The hooded figure – she only just made out the image of a blonde-haired girl – glared down at her as she screamed out. Pain shot up her leg.

"What the hell's your problem?" Kana snapped. Enough was enough. "Aren't you even going to apologise?"

Instantly the blonde tried to twist free, jerking and struggling like a trapped animal, her hood flopping back. Kana held fast. She was young, perhaps younger than Kana with piercing blue eyes, a childlike nose, and thin frowning lips. Her lack of response only riled the brunette up further.

"Did you hear me?. I --" At that point Kana noticed the bag she had dropped. Eyes narrowed, watching as crimson liquid dribbled from the carrier to the linoleum floor.

"Damn. Sumbitch." The blonde squealed and tugged harder. Still Kana held tight. However, her eyes were glued to the mess of oily red liquid oozing across the floor. For a split second she forgot about her grip.

"Is that blood?. Did you just steal blood bags?" Kana's mouth fell open.

"Let go." The girl's insisted, eyes shooting up. They landed on the camera just above them. She glared at it and then turned back to Kana. "Let go, dammit. Come on, please?" She was clearly American, Southern by her accent. It accent was dense and rolling. Kana had to focus to make out her words.

"Why are you stealing blood? What is wrong with you?"

"None of your damn business. "

"Over there." Two security guards exclaimed, rounding the corner, arms raised and pointing.

"Shit." She heard the girl growl, felt her stiffen. "Fine. Be like 'at, then."

In seconds, Kana felt herself snatched from the ground and thrust over the blonde's slim shoulder. She squealed as her leg dangled. Reeling, the girl beneath her grasp the blood-soaked bag and ran towards the exit.

"Put me down." Kana screamed, her hands fisting and slamming into the girl's back.

"Shut up." The resulting whimper from the blonde did not placate her. The inhalation of air so close to her neck froze Kana. For some reason, it felt as though she had sniffed her. An uncomfortable shiver rippled through the struggling girl. Glancing up, she could still see the girl's pursuers tearing after them.

"I'll scream if you don't put me --" Her threat was interrupted as she was thrown, bodily into the back seat of a silver Mercedes Benz. "down?" The partition hit her in the stomach as she landed, knocking the words from her.

Her leg slammed against the seat. She screamed in silent agony, the air knocked from her lungs.

3

Kana's head spun. She gasped for air. In some corner of her brain, she acknowledged the blonde climbing into the car before the lurch of the seat alerted her to its acceleration out of the car park.

Two voices rich with accents echoed from the front seats and she tried to concentrate on them, pushing away the urge to whine in her discomfort. Her leg throbbed violently and nausea burned in the back of her throat. Focusing upon the voices, she forced away the urge to pass out and drew in as much air as possible.

"You are kidnapping people now?" The female voice with a sweet trill to it, perhaps a purr of Spanish or Italian.

"She saw my face, I couldn't leave her there to talk to the cops." A third voice seemed to be moaning in pain, and it took several seconds for Kana to register that it was hers.

"Quiet." Snapped the Latin accent.

The interior temperature of the car seemed to plummet with the foreign woman's order. Goosebumps prickled on Kana arms. Pushing up on her hands, Kana saw the thermostat on the car dashboard plummet to five degrees Celsius. She did a double take. It hadn't moved.

Distracted from her pain, Kana shifted her hips, pulling herself up into a sitting position. Her leg screamed in protest, but still she fought through it. After a quick fumble for her seat belt, it clicked in easily enough.

The car interior boasted black tinted windows, and leather seating that still retained its new car smell. Even the slightest movement from her earned a squeak from the seat. Not a single crumb littered the back seat.

Finally, her eyes landed on the girl in the passenger front seat, who now stared right at Kana. Her heart skipped a beat as they locked eyes; her breath catching. The blonde narrowed her gaze, scrutinised Kana with eyes too cold and hard for her youthful face.

"Why did you not just kill her?" Soft, rich, like caramel, the voice should have been warm from the accent alone, yet the words froze Kana. She suppressed a shiver.

"I thought we meant to be keepin' a low profile." The southeastern American drawl was soothing, even if her eyes were unnerving. "Anyhow, there was a camera on the wall. If I'd killed her, I'd be in hiding for the next ten years. I tell you what, I ain't up for that. She's just a kid. And I couldn't leave her, she had a grip on me like a Miss'ippi crawdad. Oh, and she saw the blood bags."

The Spanish woman hissed something unintelligible.

Kana felt uncomfortable with this woman; she gave out an unnatural aura. Her brow furrowed, but she kept her mouth firmly shut until she gathered her senses.

"Think you might be scarin' the kid a little."

"Good." The Spanish woman distractedly replied. She sounded lost in thought.

Kana's teeth played with her bottom lip. She regretted her thoughts in the hospital cafe. She hoped she might be dreaming. The car jolted her leg. Pain reassured her of both reality and her birthday misfortune. She whined in the bottom of her throat at the pain, missing her painkillers.

"You're going to kill me, aren't you?" She asked, her voice straining for stability.

The blonde snapped around to watch her again. "Ga --"

"No." The Spanish voice interrupted. A sharp tone of warning that made Kana's stomach drop. "And you will be silent until we decide what we are to do with you."

How could she reason with them? Her Mother would never pay the ransom. If there was a ransom. Would they cut off her hair and send it through the mail if her Mother refused to pay? What about limbs? Would they cut off her fingers one by one, like in the movies? She shivered, her mind racing through a thousand possibilities, each one darker and more surreal than the last. She couldn't think straight.

Kana's gaze flicked to the passenger window as trees, fields and roads raced past at an alarming speed. She instinctively gripped the door handle. How far out of town where they taking her?

"Don't you worry none about the path," the Southern drawl reached her; the blonde giggled. "The way Gabriella here laid it out, you ain't never gonna remember the way."

This "Gabriella" clicked her tongue and Kana's stomach plummeted, instantly worried for both the American's health and her own. Had she realised she'd just used a name? Knowing her kidnappers names only put her in further danger. They would kill her, or at least, never seeing home again. She hoped for both their sake that name was an alias.

Kana slid further back into the seat wishing she could sink through it.

***

"Get out." The Spanish voice crackled through the luxurious muscle car. Kana returned to reality with a thump.

"I --"

"Now."

Kana didn't explain that she couldn't. She'd finally managed to squirm into a position where her right leg propped up properly on the seat but getting out required shifting it again.

They had finally stopped. Kana peered out of the window. A single tiny street broke the open countryside. Only seven houses could be seen for miles, spread haphazardly across the fields like a sprinkling of seeds. There was nothing else to catch the eye but yellow and green rows of fields -- too far away to identify the exact crops -- and a small farmhouse that was barely visible miles out in the distance. Trees and hedgerows sectioned off the land in organised rows. Beneath them, the paint had worn away from the pot hole strewn road.

The woman Kana now knew to be Gabriella wrenched open the back door. The click of a child lock settled any questions of trying to bail out before they reached their destination.

Finally Kana saw the Spanish woman's face clearly. Amber coloured eyes were bestial. Aquiline nose, a round mouth with cupid's bow and a firm jawline framing that frowning mouth. Her low, messy ponytail danced about her lower back in the breeze. She had flawless, olive-toned skin with a scar across her face and faint hints of wrinkles around her eyes. She wasn't that old, perhaps mid-thirties. Combat boots crunched against the ground.

With an awkward shuffle towards the door, Kana pressed her good foot to the road. The next foot she pushed down with infinite care, noting how the Spanish woman clicked her tongue impatiently.

She finally found her center of gravity, using the door as help.

"Can you walk?"

As if to answer for her, Kana winced, her hand sliding along the recently waxed chassis of the car. She toppled instantly. Gabriella lunged for her, yanked her arm, and hauled the brunette back up. Kana yelped, but it did nothing to alleviate the firm grip Gabriella had on her.

"You do not have a crutch."

"I had a wheelchair, butyour friend grabbed me andit's back at the hospital." Kana explained.

The cold woman nodded. "Come." She insisted and hoisted Kana up. The suddenness of Gabriella's actions also stole all complaint from her lips. Kana did not protest. She didn't know how her kidnappers might react to the word "no".

One hand curled around her back, the other hooked under the crook of her knees as she hoisted Kana up and lugged her towards the nearest house. Unlike Chloe, she used a little more strength; her muscles taut beneath the girl's weight. Under the woollen green jumper that scratched at Kana's skin, she felt a six pack of abdominal muscles. *Holy shit. Gabriella could snap me like a twig.*

Kana's hands awkwardly pressed against the woman's stomach, trying to avoid her chest and prevent herself from being crushed.

"Chloe. Lock the car." Gabriella bumped the car door shut with pear-shaped hips. An order. The American nodded and obliged her.

Chloe. She knew Gabriella dropped the name on purpose; a small revenge for letting her own name slip. She spied a smirk on the woman's face.

They hobbled towards the nearest house. Wooden plank walls decorated the outside, a deep chestnut in colour. The house looked warm and inviting. It was a stark contrast to the woman carrying her inside. The building looked new, but a worn mat at the front door offered a friendly " EL OME".

A sign nailed into the wood beside the door offered:

Last Chance B and B;
A Hot Meal, a Cosy Room, and Understanding.
NO MATTER WHAT YE BE

The hairs on Kana's arms prickled as she read the last line of that sign. She swore the grip around her body tightened in response. Chloe reached the door ahead of them and opened it, making room for Gabriella to cart her inside sideways.

This place was no mere kidnappers hide-out or abandoned inn. It was a glorious bed-and-breakfast. Kana stared in awe, her lips parting while she took in her surroundings. Inside, the walls were coated in a deep brown lacquer that gleamed in the light of brass lamps mounted on the walls.

The floor continued the theme of rustic opulence. Immaculate hardwood flooring was glossy enough to reflect the tiny crystal chandelier high above. Kana's gaze turned upward. She closed her mouth. If these people had money, why kidnap her?

A tiny reception booth had been renovated under the stairs with cubbyholes full of keys, letters, and an open logbook resting on top.

Kidnappers hideout by day, hotel by night? Kana laughed bitterly at the idea in her head.

Equally luxurious, the living room stretched along the entire side of the house. Through a second doorway Kana could see the kitchen.

She returned her attention to the room. Two large couches, black leather, took up at least a quarter of it, and a large flat screen television covered most of the far wall. Every other wall hosted the same brass light fixtures, as well as wooden shelves loaded with expensive looking vases, ornaments and several wall mounts loaded with muskets and rifles. An ancient grandfather clock dominated one corner and in another corner was nestled a large spider plant that reached the ceiling.

Gabriella plonked her down unceremoniously in the nearest chair.

"While I do not like to let you run around in my home," Gabriella sighed, her Spanish accent lilting slightly. "Broken leg, no clue where you are, and miles away from the city; you will not go far."

"Mum." A child-like voice crowed and Kana's head whirled. A young girl, perhaps only twelve years old, dove into the hall and tackled Gabriella, squeezing the woman tight. She had the same olive skin, same Roman nose, and the same amber eyes as Gabriella.

"Lola, shouldn't you be at school today?"

"Nope." The girl beamed. "Uncle Barney said I could come home early on account of I got gym last and I'm not allowed to take part."

"Oh. I must have forgotten." Gabriella chuckled stroking the girl's hair. Lola buried her head against her Mother's side. Kana realised just how tall she was. It wasn't often you saw a woman over six foot tall who wasn't a model. The inquisitive girl, regardless, nuzzled her and then dove at Chloe.

"Chloe. Chloe. Did you get it? Did you? Did you? Tell me." Kana peered around, curious. it was met with a tiny flicker of fear upon Gabriella's face. Clearly she hadn't expected her daughter to be around.

Kana tried to look non-threatening. It wasn't difficult given her current state.

She opened her mouth but was interrupted by Chloe who held up the blood soaked carrier bag. "Yeah, Chere, I did. I got a whole bag full of the stuff. But you better run off. Your momma and I gotta sort out a few things for our new lodger; she'll be here a while."

Lola looked at Kana, scowled just like her Mother had, and nodded before running through a doorway out of sight.

Kana watched the entire scene quietly, feeling out of place and somewhat out of time. Earlier, she'd thought she was going to die. Now they seemed to be playing happy families.

Gabriella cleared her throat.

"Now. Let me look at you." She pursed her lips. "You are just human." Kana had no idea how to respond. Gabriella backed up and sank into another chair, eyes trained on Kana. She sat forward, elbows on knees, and placed her chin in her hands. She was thinking.

"What's your name?"

"Kana."

"That is not a common name. I cannot imagine that there any many Kanas running around."

"Probably not." Kana nodded, opening up a little. She remembered reading about Lima syndrome. Perhaps she could secure her safety by creating some bond between her and her captors. "My mum and I moved here when I was a kid after my dad left us." She received a nod in reply.

"I used to live in Spain, myself." Gabriella explained. Unnecessarily, but she had a smile on her face now. Kana considered that progress. She returned it, nervously. This woman didn't need a weapon to kill her; with muscles like hers, she only needed a temper.

"Gabriella, what should we do with the girl? We gonna kill her now, or, " Chloe interrupted once more, hesitant in her asking.

Kana's eyes widened.

"No." Gabriella said firmly. "Chloe, can I ask you to please get Kana settled into a room? I think she'll like room number one zero seven. It's on the ground floor. No stairs." She gave a tiny chuckle.

"Wait, " Kana protested. She had hoped to earn more progress. Perhaps even learn something about them.

"Upsie-daisy." Instead Chloe grabbed her and bundled her over her shoulder like a sack of potatoes, carting her off into the hall. She dropped Kana on a bed in one of the rooms off the main hallway.

"Listen here, Chere." She said, her hand reaching for the door handle. "We don't really want to hurt you. But there's some explainin' to be done. That might take a while."

"Please, just let me go. I promise I won't call the police. " Kana begged, feeling crestfallen. Chloe merely shook her head with a sad look on her face.

"Sorry, darlin'. No can do." She pulled the door closed behind her leaving Kana alone with her thoughts.

4

The decor in the bedroom was sparse but it was still a step up from Kana's own bedroom. A double bed took up half of the small room, pressed up against a ground floor window. Peering outside she could see only a five foot fence.

Though she could not fathom why she had been kidnapped only to be brought to a hotel, a twisted idea sneaked into her head. *What if, they're planning to paint the walls of a room in blood and leave my corpse as a tourist attraction?*

The macabre fantasy grew in its twisted appeal, and only succeeded in giving Kana cold chills. Surely she could reason with her kidnappers, somehow. A small yet tricky journey limping across the carpet to reach the door revealed it was locked from the outside. Hearing footsteps, she stiffened and held her breath till they passed.

Without anything else to do, Kana lay down on the bed. Time drifted by. Day and night and another day passed. Occasionally, someone paused outside the door. Once she heard an off key rendition of a sea chantey float past along with footsteps, but whoever hummed it did not open the door.

"Let me go home." She muttered only to herself, not daring to let herself be heard. Huddled up inside the room for two stubborn days, hunger clawed at her senses.

Lying quietly with her thighs and arms clamped tightly around her pillow provided flimsy relief against the anxious ache in her stomach. Kana wondered if they were waiting for her to break, or worse still; perhaps they had forgotten her. She spent most of her time sleeping, her eyes puffy with tears, her face red and damp and pressed against the cool pillow she hugged so tightly.

Dehydration and lack of food had her stumbling and clumsy. Purple and yellow tracers dogged her vision, but the wall guided her toward the door. She banged on in without result, then fell asleep again leaning against it. The next time Kana woke, she heard voices outside her door. Far more lucid, for the moment, her brain processed the words with ease.

"She has to eat, Chloe."

"Give her time."

"Time for what? She hasn't eaten in two days. If she has much more time, we'll have to bury her corpse in the garden. Go, fetch me the skeleton key, I will check on her." There was no doubt in Kana's mind they were talking about her. She hobbled back to the bed and sat down.

The door creaked open slowly. Gabriella entered carrying a tray of food. Kana's stomach growled. Clicking the door closed behind her, she   immediately walked over and gently eased the tray onto the bed.

A small plate of toast sat in the center, surrounded by a steaming mug of hot water with a tea bag inside, a small jug of milk, and a tiny bowl just big enough for the six sugar cubes it held. The tray also held another small plate of miniature preserves; strawberries jam, raspberry jam, marmalade, and tiny corners of butter in silver foil. She nodded to Kana to eat. A knife and a spoon hid inside a paper napkin in the side.

"I must apologize; I had not intended to leave you so long. We were unavoidably entangled in some matters outside the house. I hope you're not too hungry."

"I'm starved, actually."

"Then eat, please."

Despite Kana's whisper of worry that it could be poisoned, she dived into the spreads and immediately began adding preserves. The first bite was like ambrosia on her empty stomach and only spurred her to finish every last bite. Gabriella spoke while Kana wolfed down her first meal in days.

"We have come to a conclusion. I mean Chloe, myself, and the others. We won't kill you. You'll be glad to know." She offered Kana an uneasy smile, but Kana only wiped the crumbs from her mouth with her arm. Determined not to indicate any weakness by letting her relief show, Kana simply sat stone-faced and let the woman continue. "But we must keep you here with us for a while. Get to know us. We're not really bad people, you know. We're just different."

"So you won't leave me to die as a corpse in here?"

"What?" The Spanish woman looked confused. "Dios mio, no. What must you think of us? We will look after you. Think of it as free room and board, perhaps?"

But she couldn't. Kana shook her head.

"Look, thanks for the food, but my mother's probably worried about me." She doubted this, herself, but her captor did not need to know that. "Please, you have to take me home. I promise I won't tell anyone anything."

The door opened slightly, and someone Kana hadn't yet met stood in the doorway. While Gabriella stood tall, with firm muscle, this man stood taller still; the height difference gave him an almost gaunt appearance. His green eyes glimmered in the light and watched her with cruel interest. He had black hair was shaved back in a buzz cut and his angular jaw jutted forward enough to make his entire appearance unnerving.

He wore a long trench coat, buttoned to the top. His feet were shrouded in heavy steel-toed boots that peeked out from under loose black jeans. He eyed Kana icily, but Gabriella shooed him away with a wave of her hand.

The stranger shook his head and beckoned her closer.

"Un Segundo, " Gabriella muttered, rising swiftly to her feet and crossing the room. The wraithlike figure leant close and whispered in her ear. Kana noted how she flinched when he almost pressed his lips against her ear.

"No." Gabriella replied sharply.

"At least consider it. It will solve many a problem before it reaches a dangerous peak." The stranger shot Kana a dark look.

"I believe I just said no. Gracias, Barney, but it is not a problem." Gabriella sighed and turned to Kana who had paused in eating, staring curiously at them. Barney seemed even stranger than the other two. The look he shot her sparked anger and revulsion in Kana.

"If you're talking about me being here," Kana said with more venom in her tone that she had originally intended. "I want to go home. How's that for solving a problem?"

The man's jaw jutted forward and his eyebrows lowered. Kana felt the colour drain from her face.

"You know nothing about this place, you little brat. If you knew what was good for you, you'd shut your mouth and your eyes, and maybe Gabriella will let you go home." He snarled the words at her, and Kana felt the same bubbling anger stew inside her that she did when her mother was around.

If she could have stood, she would have. Instead, Kana tugged her lip up into a sneer and retorted. "Are you what happens when she says no, Barney, was it? Like the purple dinosaur? Because all I hear is rawr, rawr, rawr."

"You repugnant little wretch."

Gabriella blinked and looked between the two of them for several seconds. Kana could not read her blank expression until she closed her eyes and sighed. Exasperation.

"Enough." She said firmly. "Kana, eat your toast, Barney, I need a word with you, in private." She grabbed the taller man by the sleeve of his leather jacket and tugged him from the room. The door slammed.

Kana breathed out a sigh of relief. Left to eat the remainder of the toast in peace, she sniffed the tea – it smelled like normal tea – and promptly prepared it exactly how she liked it. Milky, with two sugars. She pressed the bag to the side of the cup to strain it and spooned it onto the crumb covered plate. The hot liquid brought a calming sigh up from the depths of her body. She couldn't remember her last cup of tea, but the tangy sweetness was enough to help her regain her senses.

Maybe Gabriella wasn't quite the ice queen she seemed in the car. Perhaps something had gone awry there. Kana relaxed on the bed, making a mental note to inquire as to the reason for the blood theft.

A child's laughter broke her thoughts, a bubbly voice that Kana vaguely remembered to be Gabriella's daughter. She appeared in the open doorway wearing a thin, yellow summer dress that reached mid-calf and seemed to swirl of its own accord. Her legs were bare and mud had dried on her feet and up her ankles. Feathers spiked from the young girl's hair, canary yellow in colour, and her hair was just as bright blonde. Her eyes twinkled, a pastel purple. She held a thin knot of string in her hand that she twirled around. On the end of it was a key. Kana's gaze locked onto the key. If she had it, and was here, where was Gabriella and Chloe? ?

"Mum said I could stay off school today because you're here, but I have to be really, really good." She flashed Kana a grin.

Kana nodded blankly. She closed her eyes again, lazily, but the pop of bubble gum snapped Kana's attention back to the pre-teen.

"Uncle Barney says you're a lazy lump of flesh because you sleep past noon."

Kana closed her eyes tighter and drew in another long, deep breath. She ran her hands through her tangled brunette hair. Hang on, past noon? Her eyes snapped open and she sat up, but the room had no clocks. Time locked inside this room was warped and stood still, with only the rising and setting of the sunlight that came through the window to indicate the world beyond was moving forward.

"Mum yells at me when I sleep past noon."

"Mm hm." Kana eyes would stay shut this time.

"Mum didn't yell at you. She must like you better."

Kana said nothing in response and only pulled the covers around her tighter.

"Uncle Barney doesn't like you."

Uncle. The kid called that intolerable leather-loving freak Uncle.

The thought tugged Kana's upper lip up in disgust.

"I don't think much of him, either, if I'm honest." She paused. Maybe she should curb her language around the kid. If he did turn out to be her Uncle, it wouldn't do well to belittle him in front of her; who knows, he might actually be a half decent Uncle. Still, the temptation was too much: "The way I see it, he can go and never mind."

"What?" The child pressed.

"Nothing."

"Go and what?"

"Yes. Do tell. Barney can go and what?" A rich baritone rumble rolled into the room, twisting Kana's stomach with a start. With long, heavy strides, Barney's wiry frame glided into view. He entered the room and placed a tender, leather gloved hand protectively on Lola's shoulder. Another bubble popped in the girl's mouth.

Kana forced a grin.

"You can discuss room arrangements with Gabriella." She improvised, her tone brimming with more sarcasm than she liked.

"Is that so?" Barney's nostrils flared over a sour smirk. "Lola, why not go outside and play before your Mother calls you? I'm sure I heard her talking about introducing another chore."

"Aww." The inquisitive girl whined and spun around to leave. Kana gripped the bed sheets, uncomfortable being left alone with him. "Hey Lola, why not stay inside and keep me company instead?"

"Oh, sure, like I'll listen to you. Yeah, right." Lola bolted from the room and Kana scrambled to sit near the headboard, putting distance between herself and the intrusive man. Her right leg dragged uselessly in the cast. Barney licked his top lip slowly and tsked, looking around the room casually. His gaze settled on the bedside lamp and he curled the pull string around his index finger.

Light illuminated the shadowy room.

"So, good morning." Kana attempted to be civil.

Uncle Barney dropped the cord, moved in much too close and put a gloved hand under her chin and tilted her head up toward him. Chartreuse green eyes pierced into her.

"Don't touch me." She grit her teeth and pulled away. He grasped her again, gripping her jaw tight till she was forced to part her lips.

"You're pathetic." The words were unprovoked, yet he sneered at her. She tried to bat his hand away but he was faster and gripped her wrist tight in his other hand. Kana grimaced, unable to unset her mouth lest it hurt even more. "I said, you're pathetic. Look at you. Broken leg. Scared. Shivering. You don't belong here with us. Petty mortal, I should put you out of your misery."

As frightening as this man was, obviously unhinged, even; petty mortal, what was that? Kana's temper was equal to her fear. Who was this man? Who did he think he was?. His grip on her wrist tightened and she gripped the bed sheets with her other one. The creaking of his leather gloves broke the silence in the room.

"Let go of me, you fucking freak!" Kana jerked, causing enormous pain. She couldn't stop herself from yelling. A shrill squeal escaped her as his fierce grip crushed her thin wrist. As she fought, his lips contorted into a disgusted sneer. Big bad Barney was enjoying this. "You sick monster. Is this how you get your kicks?"

"You don't learn, do you?" His grip impossibly tightened.

"Stop it. I said let go." She gulped in air, straining in pain.She squealed, her words muffled through his grip on her jaw. The harder she fought, his hands tightened even more. Kana felt bones shift inside her arm. He was going to snap her wrist.. "Stop."

His hand released her face, and then it slapped her hard across her cheek.

"You don't tell me what to do, Kara."

"It's Kana – Ahh, that hurts." He reacted to her correction by digging his nails into her crushed wrist. Any more and it would snap. "You stupid jerk," she hissed through gritted teeth.

He lifted her up, forcing her body up off the bed. The tea-tray went flying, her tea soaking the sheets, crumbs flying across the floor. Crockery clinked. She pivoted on her good leg while the broken one dangled at an awkward angle. The tug of the cast weighing down the unhealed bones and a current of sharp pain shot up through the injury.

She breathed heavy, tears gathering in her eyes. The blanket slipped from her waist. Kana let it.

"Your stay here is short, you stupid bitch." His words, though whispered smooth and deep, rasped hot in her ear and made her cringe. "You don't belong here. You stay away from us, especially Gabriella, or else."

"Barney," a calmer voice spoke from the doorway, "will you let go, please, darlin'? I think the girl needs some rest. You should probably oughta put her down, by 'n' by."

Her attacker snarled, low and feral, his green eyes focused only on Kana's face.

Chloe took several steps deeper into the bedroom, arms raised in a calming motion. How long had she been lurking in the hall? Barney turned on the American. His expression was chilling. Chloe slowly retreated a step. "Ah, I was just suggesting perhaps you might wanna continue your conversation later? You're scaring her."

Barney dropped Kana onto the floor, jarring her leg again. She let out another squeal and clutched at her injured leg, doubling up. Pain ricocheted up her tailbone, and she rolled onto her side for relief, narrowly missing a plate.

"Oh, I'm scaring her? Chloe, I suggest you leave the room and I'll pretend I didn't hear you. Just because I can't kill you, doesn't mean I can't hurt you." Barney dragged his fingers along the bedside lamp and smirked.

Kana tried to massage her aching wrist. A rapidly purpling thick band resembling a handprint slowly darkened around her crushed skin.

"You don't want to be here, and you shouldn't be." He was literally talking down to Chloe now. Kana sat on the floor, wishing she could disappear. He turned to her, his face expressionless. She swallowed slowly. "I'm not stupid. Neither are you. This is not the kind of house you belong in."

"W-what?"

"Barney." Chloe growled, actually sounding fearsome. "You heard what Gabriella said. She is gonna be furious with you.." Barney backed away slowly, as though considering, and Kana remembered how to breath. "And don't forget why you're here. You can hurt me, but do you really want to find out if I can hurt you back? Might be I can,"

"You think so?" With a flash of movement, Barney wrenched the lamp from the bedside table and smacked the blonde American across the head with it. Chloe staggered to the floor.

"What are you doing?." Kana erupted.

"Shut up," he snarled, .you're not worth the blood smear on the walls.." He slammed down the lamp still clenched in his fist. It shattered on impact with the thin blue carpet. With a snort of derision, he stormed out of the room.

Kana didn't move, paralysed with shock, anchored to the spot. She peered down at the whimpering mess on the floor.

"Chloe, are you okay?" Kana tentatively reached out. Kidnapper or not, she felt sorry for her. The crack of the lamp hitting her still echoed in her ears. "Thanks for trying to help. You didn't have to."

The word karma raced through Kana's mind.

Chloe moaned on the floor, clutching her head. Kana found her feet, with the help of the wall and slid closer. From this new angle she could see a gaping hole in the blonde's hair, and blood. So much blood. Kana wasn't squeamish, but the blood flowed so free and thick that even she had to recoil.

"Gabriella, ." she screamed at the top of her lungs. The name was loud, sharp and booming throughout the house, the years of shouting and bawling between her Mother and herself had built up her voice.

Gabriella came running instantly.

"What's happened?" The Spanish woman's eyes rapidly flicked from the downed American to the shattered lamp and tea set soaking the bed and finally to the upturned plate and tea tray on the floor.

She pointing at the writhing blonde.

Gabriella rolled her eyes as if Kana were being ridiculous. "She's fine."

" No, she is hurt, bad... Barney smashed her in the head."

Gabriella clicked her tongue and frowned. She then wheeled Kana around and forced her to look at the hole in Chloe's head.

"Look."

Kana did. The blood around the wound had already begun to thicken, to turn black. She pulled a face and tried to look away but Gabriella's hands wrapped around her head keeping it still. The woman's grip was strong. Her efforts to turn were futile. From the toned appearance of Gabriella, she could see her snapping her neck, possibly accidentally.

"She needs a hospital."

Gabriella said nothing. Kana focused. She swore the wound looked smaller now. Perhaps it had just been a superficial injury. At least the bleeding had stopped.The wound contracted visibly, the blood congealing. It matted the blonde hair against her head, but the skin beneath continued to re-knit as she watched.

"That's impossible.".

Gabriella chuckled, a trill of laughter like the trickle of a stream. Chloe was moving now. Still hunched over on the floor, she shook her head hard, making her blonde hair fly. Kana couldn't see her face but clearly heard a low growl that sent an icy chill up her spine.

"What the hell?"

"Now, move." Gabriella shouted as she pulled Kana to one side and shoved her hard out of the room towards the hall. The captive was finally free, but she crashed against the hallway wall, almost crumpled as her casted right leg bore all her weight for five whole seconds. She spun round. Chloe had jumped to her feet, snarling.

What fresh hell was this?

Kana backed up against the wall, as the American girl grabbed Gabriella with both hand and tore into her neck with her teeth. A thin splatter of blood sprayed over Chloe's face, highlighting eyes that had gone silver and manic.

Kana's scream caught in her throat. She hobbled quickly towards the front door with all the speed she could muster, pressed close against the wall for its support. She could still hear the thick slurping noise of Chloe's mouth against Gabriella's neck. Drowning it out, Kana repressed the insistent overturning inside her stomach and kept moving. Her casted leg thunked, useless to support her weight. Fear rising, she resorted to dragging it behind her, hopping on the other. Despite the burning ache screaming up her shin, she had to get out of here.

Curse her rotten luck.

She reached the front door, wrenched it open, and kept going. Her cast scraped the ground as she headed for the gate.

Except there was no seeing any gate. Instead something massive, hunched, and hairy stood right in her path, something that growled with the rumbling ferocity of a freight train.

Kana backed up a little, and forgot how to breathe.

It was the size of a lion, and dwarfed the gate behind it. Its lips withdrew into a black and yellow sneer on a muzzle long and twitching. Kana could see her panicked expression reflecting in the void black of its eyes.

It had to be a wolf. Or part bear.

"N-nice puppy," Kana squeaked out, her voice unsteady. Her knuckles whitened as she gripped the railing of the sign. Fingernails dug into the wood.

It lunged. Kana screamed. Her voice echoed out across the wide open countryside. She fell backward with an awkward thump, straining her broken leg again. She sobbed at her impending death and scrunched watering eyes tight, feeling wetness on her cheeks, but she dared not look at the monster.

Shaking, Kana waited for the impact and the inevitable bite.

Still, she waited.

Yet her death didn't come. She felt him hovering over her body. Then the beast's heat fell over the top of her, his shaggy warmth smothering. Her limbs curled up tight like a startled spider, hands pressed against her face. She could smell the hot raw stench of its most recent meal, a rank door that poured between her fingers with each rumbling breath. Her own came out in gasps. A massive paw lifted up and pressed against her stomach, pinning her.

Still she did not dare open her eyes.

Only a quarter of its weight pressed down upon her, the tips of its claws poking easily through her t-shirt. It was the same t-shirt from the day she broke her leg, dowsed now in sweat from fear.

"Don't eat me," she breathed out slowly. She just wanted to go home, back to her mother; her shouting yet predictable mother, her oblivious and caustic mother, who had never given much of a damn. At least the woman never tried to maim or kill her, despite her hateful urges. Kana didn't want her last conscious memory to be the lining of a wolf's throat.

She still hadn't opened her eyes when she felt a second paw on her. She squealed again, expecting the creature to rip her chest open and dig in. Her breath hitched as she sobbed. To hell with dignity, she'd cry if she wanted to. The beast, inexplicably, pawed at her like a kneading kitten. While not painful, it was uncomfortable and terrifying. The weight, pushing down, squeezed the air from her lungs.

Finally he stopped.

Kana stopped crying.

An age seemed to pass before she found the courage to force open her eyes. Onyx orbs stared back, a coal black nose sniffed deeply and rapidly at her body and face. Fur lined white lips were peeled back from thick black gums to reveal a sticky pink tongue. Oh, god. Was it going to lick her? Kana held her breath for an eternity. Her gaze flicked to her chest where claws shone like meat hooks. A crackling growl from the wolf pulled his thin lips further back, revealing sharp blades of teeth.

She was terrified. She lay there pinned to the ground by the giant canine creature. Finally, the growling stopped and Kana realised she was shaking from head to toes. The paws bent forward and the beast knelt, now lying on top of her, as if getting comfortable.

She blinked, startled and confused.

It yawned and Kana finally let her hands move, reaching up to pat its head with infinite care. The wolf readjusted and curled up on top on her, both pinning her and drowning her in heat.

"Oh no no, don't." She whimpered, still shaking with fear, but she shoved the beast's massive head trying to make it move. Nothing. She pushed harder. Still nothing.

At least her casted leg remained free of the beast's weight, almost as though the lupine beast had taken care to avoid that part of her, and that part alone. Once more, she tried to shift the beast, his head turned around, staring at her. Its maw hung open, tongue lolling out how dogs do when they are happy. Kana gagged at its breath as it snorted, almost like a laugh, but the stench of a million raw meals wafted into her face.

Well, at least he wasn't eating her.

"Vincent." Gabriella shouted from the doorway and Kana had to do a double take. The woman had a towel pressed to her neck. Wait, wasn't she busy with bleeding to death in the bedroom? "Get off her, bad, bad, You move now.."

The beast backed up, getting off her sprawled out body. Relieved to be free, Kana sat up and watched as the beast began to shed. There was a series of violent cracks, the beast contorting, until finally he began to resemble something like a human.

"What the fuck is going on?" Kana yelled. She scrambled back, crawling like a crab but Gabriella's icy gaze stopped her. Looking at both Kana and the man, she shook her head.

"That Cabrón, is Vincent."

5

"I hope you're all proud of yourselves." Gabriella's stern tone echoed through the sitting room. "Is this how you behave in public? Can I trust none of you to behave? Do I have to throw you all out and let you fend for yourselves like common strays? Dios mio." Her hand slammed down on the coffee table. "This is a safe house, not a den of stupidity."

Kana huddled on the living room couch, complete with blanket to stop the shivers, but she noticed the guilty faces in the group. Gabriella was like a school teacher scolding a group of nought children. Chloe stared down at her shoes. Barney sulked. But the third person with a stubble-dusted face was scowling out of the window with zero apparent interest.

This new face belonged to Vincent.

Kana's gaze lingered on him. He seemed to sense it and turned to meet her gaze with azure eyes that matched her own. He had a

43

square jaw with blonde scruff adorned his chin and upper lip. His mouth parted in a rakish grin when he caught her looking. His hair was overgrown and dragged across his shoulders, a faded blond in colour. Even now, the only word that floated into Kana's mind to describe the man was 'wolfish', her brain unable to blot out the events preceding Gabriella helping her back inside.

She gave him a withering glare, turned away. When she dared a tiny glance, he was still looking. She returned to watching Gabriella, whose expression, although still quite stern, had eased slightly.

"Chloe, I can just about understand. But two hundred years is more than enough to learn how to behave in front of mortals. Regardless of injury, you ask first.If you cannot handle that simple rule, then you put everyone at risk. Slip again and I will stake you myself."

Chloe hissed her discontent. Gabriella fired a warning glare. Kana noticed the fangs just before they disappeared and finally put two and two together.

Blood bags, biting Gabriella's neck, and the fangs.

"You're a vampire." she exclaimed. "And you, " she pointed at Vincent. "You're a werewolf? What kind of hell have I fallen into?" Everyone ignored her shocked name-calling, except Vincent, who snickered.

Clearly, the wolf had a sense of humour.

Gabriella rounded on Vincent now. He loped across the room to slump into the chair across from Kana who was, by now, failing to process anything else. Barney suddenly looked interested and leaned forward in his seat. Vincent looked smug.

"Vincent Morgan."

"Aye, love?"

"Really?" Gabriella's voice dripped with disdain.

"What?" That was a strong Welsh accent. That very accent along with that arrogant smugness boiled Kana's blood. She wanted Gabriella to smack him across the face.

Gabriella narrowed her eyes, but she stayed her hand, and leaned over him, hands coverin his that lay upon the armrests. Suddenly a flash of ice moulded both pairs of hands to the chair. The frozen liquid seemed to sprout straight from the woman's fingertips and crackle as it spread across Vincent's wrists hardening into jagged crystals.

Kana stared in blank confusion.

The wolf man sat up now, taunting, his face inches from Gabriella's curvy chest. He tugged at the ice uselessly. The woman's eyes shone darkly.

"I always said you had nice tits, Gabby," he grinned. "But ye needn't go to such trouble to get my eyes on 'em."

"Shut up." The words burst from Kana.

Gabriella turned, raising an eyebrow in amusement. Chloe's smile appeared as she peered over, giggling. Even Barney seemed to be fighting an amused sneer.

"I don't care how clever you think you are." Kana drove on, the words tumbling from her lips, "You pounced on me while .you were some sort of a god damned wolf, sitting on my chest like a stinky sheepdog with razor claws. You meant to terrify me. You did it on purpose, .now you're sitting there like a smug lecher. How dare you."

Vincent's mouth blossomed into a generous grin. Kana's face flushed hot with fury. How dare he grin. .If not for her broken leg, she would love to stand up, walk over there and slap the stupid off his face..

"Aye lass, it's true. I meant to scare the bloody pants off ya." He chuckled with a naughty wink. Kana clenched her fists. Gabriella ripped her hands free from the ice, leaving Vincent's trapped. She pulled back and punched him hard, right in the center of his smug face. He recoiled at first, but even Kana flinched at the resulting growl. Yes. Apparently he did mean it that way.

"Vincent, you will not touch that girl again. If you want to stay here, you will --"

"Easy, easy, ." Vincent snarled, "I barely touched the lass. And where's my thank you for stopping her running away while you were getting yourself gnawed on like a chew toy?"

Gabriella paused. Kana noted the wide eyed look she gave Vincent and how the Spanish woman looked ready to start shouting. Instead, she thrust a long finger in Kana's direction, and silence descended. Gabriella's finger pointed to her cast.

"What the hell do you call that?" Gabriella's retort spat out like battery acid, yet Vincent still smirked.

"A lass with a gorgeous set of legs; well at least one, I can't see the other one. " He frowned, watching the ice climb further up his arms. Gabriella clicked her tongue with impatience.

"I have had it up to here with you all. For years we've been here with no problems." Her accent had thickened in her irritation. "If you can't control yourselves, and God knows some of you aren't even trying."

"She doesn't belong here with us." Barney interjected with malice.

"How come I get frozen to a poxy chair just for sitting on her, and a punch in the face for that matter," Vincent whined, "but Miss Jaws gets to turn you into Sunday lunch and all she gets is a 'tsk tsk'?"

Gabriella twirled as if on a swivel.

"Chloe will be seen to accordingly. Either way, Barney provoked her, she needed blood to heal, and you are a *grano en el culo.*"

"Noted."

"For that matter, Barney precipitated this whole *puto desastre.* Did you read the sign in front, *pendejo?* It says 'no matter what ye be'. *Comprende?* No matter what."

Vincent still wore that self-assured smirk, and Kana still wanted to slap it off despite Gabriella's punch. She wanted the pleasure of doing it herself. In fact, since his hands were bound, she might as well. She tried to stand, and all eyes fell upon her. A cold chill lay heavy in the air. Never mind. Kana slipped back in her seat. She felt ridiculous; the victim of some cruel joke. Trapped here with a vampire, a werewolf, an ice queen and Barney, whatever crazy monster he turned out to be.

The conversation continued. Gabriella began ranting in Spanish, directed at Barney, who merely sat and nodded in a bored manner; his fingertips tapping together. Gabriella, sensing this, turned sharp, and met his line of sight.

"Don't even start, *Carajo,* I know you don't like her here, but taking her back is no longer an option, and no one gets killed in my house unless *I* say. *Gracias.*" Gabriella's fingers reached up to pinch the bridge of her nose.

Kana's eyes found Vincent's. He winked and grinned. She threw him a disgusted look. He laughed out loud, so she smirked to show she thought he was stupid and turned away.

He chuckled lightly, unfazed. "Hola, Gabby, if you could turn the heating up, I'll get out of your hair. As scintillating as your conversation is, it's all going right over my head."

Gabriella rolled her eyes and waved him off, not even turning to look at him. The ice splintered instantly, spraying across the room like shattered glass. Some shards dug into his skin. The wolf man's blue eyes dilated, his nostrils flared, and Kana swore she saw the stubble on his face thicken. As he stood, plucking out loose ice, the wounds closed immediately just as Chloe's had. Apparently everyone had some form of unnaturally fast healing. Kana looked down at her broken leg and cursed it, feeling jealous.

Vincent strode over to Kana unhindered now. She stiffened, leaning back and gave him an uneasy look. If he came closer, his arms free or not, she would slap him. She found him rude, coarse, and his long blonde hair made him look scruffy, exactly the kind of man her Mother would find abhorrent. For once, they could agree on such a thing.

Vincent leaned closer, giving her a soft smile. Kana wrinkled her nose. The strong smell of marijuana billowed from him.

"You know, lass, I didn't exactly mean to frighten you that much. Just thought Gabriella would be rather pissed if I let you run off." His voice was quiet, meant just for her. "I was aware of everything, even the way your heartbeat sped up." Then he had the nerve to wink. "Wouldn't mind having you under me again."

Crack.

The room grew deathly quiet and Kana felt she had just broken her hand. She shook the numbing pain from it. Everyone turned to look as the red welt appeared on Vincent's cheek.

The entire world seemed to freeze. Chloe was the first to break the silence with a long trickle of laughter. Vincent's jaw tightened, but his eyes danced. His gaze, a breath away was soft, almost puppy-like.

Kana wanted to stab them. Instead, she sat perfectly still, face-to-face, daring him to say something else crude. Gabriella smirked. She walked over, placed a hand on Kana's shoulder. She felt protected.

"You were leaving, Vincent." Gabriella reminded the wolf man. Her voice was thick with amusement.

"Sorry?" Kana said, more to the muscular woman than to Vincent. Gabriella shook her head and continued to laugh.

"Don't be, not for this *hijo de putana*."

While Kana didn't exactly know what that meant, she could pretty much guess. She met the golden gaze of the Spanish woman, finally examining her in detail. Her eyes shone with mirth.

Her face would have been utterly beautiful except for the long white scar that split her chin and bottom lip. It was nasty, grey, and thin making Gabriella's smirk tug the skin around it.

Kana wondered how someone could possible scar an ice queen.

Vincent whistled a long flat note, breaking the tension. He softened his expression, straightened up, and crackled his knuckles in a show of strength. "Aye. I'm going out." He stalked away and the front door slammed behind him. "Hah." Chloe trilled a delighted laugh. "Well, that weren't no daisy.." Her accent was oddly refreshing after Vincent's thick brogue.

"Chloe." Gabriella snapped, stopping the laughter, while still looking Kana in the eye. She crouched down to her level, her gaze feeling motherly and almost kind now. "That was incredibly brave, and twice as stupid."

"I know. I really am sorry."

"I can't have you hitting our guests, even if they act like idiots. You understand me?" Kana nodded in agreement. "I think today is the day when I have to tell everyone that rule again."

"Yeah, I know. He was just," Kana couldn't think of a nice word.

"Arrogant?"

"Yeah." She completely agreed.

"And sleazy?"

"Yes, my thoughts exactly."

Barney coughed loudly and stood up, wearing his trademark frown. "When you're done mollycoddling the pathetic human, Gabriella, I'll be in my room," He gave Kana a sneer. "And thank you *so* much for that lovely sermon about touching the girl."

Someone knocked on the front door.

It earned a frustrated growl from Barney. Kana's looked toward the living room doorway. She realized people would be checking it at all times at a Bed and Breakfast.

Surely there were other humans around here. No wonder Gabriella needed her more exotic guests to behave. If things got out of hand like this all the time, it could be messy. Hopefully none of the other human guests had seen Vincent as a wolf.

Gabriella pointed at Chloe, then at Barney, then finally at Kana.

"No one moves until I get back." She warned the three of them, walking into the hallway. Kana glanced at her feet. Barney sighed audibly and Chloe nibbled on her nails. No one made eye contact.

"I swear, Vincent, if you've forgotten your key, " Gabriella's muttered words were followed by the sound of the door creaking open.

"Hello," Came a cheerful flutter of a voice. Warm, but tiny, like a child's. "I'm looking for a room."

"I'm sorry, but I'm afraid we are," Gabriella, out of sight, searched for a word, then settled on, "occupado. No space at all."

Kana's brows narrowed. That was a straight out lie. She had only a handful of people around and it was a big place. Perhaps they only took in non-humans. She listened, her neck straining to see.

"Oh, but oh dear."

"I am sorry." The door started to close, creaking as it did.

"Wait please, " the squeak of her voice protested, shrill and sudden. " I'm looking for a Gabriella Montez. Do you know if she's around here?"

Another creak as the door opened again.

"Gabriella Montigo?"

"Yes, that's the name. You know her? She runs a hotel around here and I heard she takes in," she whispered the last word loudly, "Strays." Kana leaned forward in her seat, listening even more intently. This little girl sounded about eight, nine at most. Kana pictured her looking positively adorable.

"Speaking." Gabriella declared.

"Oh thank Goodness. I need somewhere to stay, are you certain you have no more rooms?" The childlike voice rose in pitch though not in volume as a frantic note edged into it. "Please, the weather man said there would be rain and well, I can't be in rain. Please."

"Si, si. Come in. Miss ?"

"Yula. Yula Ma Ril. I'm a --"

"Shhh, wait. Let us get inside first, I have neighbours."

"Oh yes." A slight gasp, "Yes, of course. Inside. Yes." The girl fussed.

With the soft tapping of footfalls, the pair re-emerged into view. Kana's brows rose. Short, yes, but definitely no child; the newcomer flittered into view, curiously looking at everything.

The newcomer looked exceedingly flustered. Her round face reddened as she realised everyone had been listening to her. Kana peered curiously. Why had Gabriella changed her mind?

Kana had never seen such a brilliant shade of red hair before. That vibrant vermilion could not be possible in nature, but the girl wearing it did not seem bold enough to pull off dyed hair. It had been cropped short, resting just above her shoulders and swept back from her face in a brown headband. Equally red eyebrows confirmed her natural redhead state. Even the girl's freckles were maroon sprinkled ing across her tiny, pointed lily white nose and cheeks.

She a simple, sandy-brown dress that was a little on the short side, even for her diminutive height. She was no child, the dress cradled pear shaped hips. Her mud caked feet were bare andas pale as the rest of her, shone against the hardwood floor. She could only be four foot ten at most.

"Hello." She offered, warily looking at each person. "Sorry, I didn't mean to interrupt." Gabriella appeared from behind and placed a gentle hand upon her shoulder. The girl all but leapt into the air at the unexpected touch.

"It's alright," she reassured. "Come in and take a seat. Chloe, will you make her a cup of tea?" Chloe turned to go into the kitchen.

"No, please.." The girl squeaked, her hands darting out in panic and she shook her head frantically. "No-no-no. Sorry, I can't. Do you have anything stronger? Like whiskey? I can't drink tea, it's too weak. Too much water, so sorry."

Kana quirked a brow. The waifish thing looked like tea would knock her arse over tit, let alone whiskey. Gabriella shrugged, and looked at Barney. He gave a brief nod.

"I have some bourbon in the top cupboard. She is welcome to it." He stated, smiling at the red head. She giggled, blushed again, and bit her nail, turning her hips from side to side.

Kana's mouth twisted in distaste. Was this girl putting it on? And how. But Kana supposed if she were as tiny and adorable, she'd probably use the same excuse to extort things from people.

"Thank you so much." Yula smiled. To Kana's complete shock, Barney beckoned her over, rising from his seat to invite her to sit.

"Come and take a seat beside me. What are you, a kinetic?"

"Oooh goodness no. Nothing so droll." She tittered out a laugh, waving her hand as she flounced into the seat. "A kinetic," Kana blurted. "What's that?"

The redhead turned, as if finally noticing her sitting in the chair and blinked in curiosity. Her mouth opened in an "o", before bouncing out of the seat and fluttering over. She bent over, staring, far too deep into Kana's personal space. She blinked and leant back, surprised by her sudden invasion of her privacy. Barney glared. Kana imagined he wished to break her other leg.

"She's a human. You've got a human." She squeaked, pointing right in her face. Her finger was inches from her nose. Yula looked at Gabriella. "I heard you didn't take in humans."

Kana felt sheer bewilderment. She must have missed something. "Wait, aren't *you* human?"

Yula shook her head vehemently. "Haha, no, no no. I'm a salamander. *You're* a human."

"Yes, I know *I* am." The confusion remained, just as thick. Gabriella smirked from the doorway, leaning against it, her shoulders shaking as she tried to hide a laugh. Kana shot her a look of "help me," but the woman remained exactly where she stood.

"I've never seen one up close. Wow. It looks so normal. Bit drab, maybe" She pushed back Kana's fringe bangs to see her forehead, and Kana instantly recoiled, pushing the girl away from her.

"Whoa, personal space." She snapped out, hating being pawed at like some zoo animal. "I'm a human yes, but I'm not a pet. Don't touch me."

Barney snarled and stalked over, a leather-clad hand landing on Yula's shoulder, ushering her back to her seat. Kana heard her whisper, "Human. They've actually got one, " to Barney who grunted in response.

As Yula settled back down into the chair, her eyes still trained on Kana, Chloe wandered back through with a grin of her own and a small glass of amber coloured liquid. The vampire had been so quiet, Kana hadn't noticed her leave the room. Clearly she'd heard everything.

"Yula, is it?" Gabriella asked, head tilting, just before the blonde vampire handed her the glass. "Sorry to ask, but given the circumstances, I must be certain: You are over eighteen, please? Licensing laws and such, I don't much care to get my ass handed to me."

"Oh no." Yula giggled, grinning wide. "No, I mean yes, I'm definitely over eighteen. Very over." She shuffled into a cross-legged position, dress covering just what it needed to and no more. "I'm a salamander. I've been alive since, " She counted on her fingertips, "Which one of your years is this?"

"How can you not know what year it is?" Kana blurted out in her confusion.

"Shut up, human." Barney growled, the others ignored her, shaking their heads in disdain at her question.

"It's two thousand and sixteen on their dominant calendar." Gabriella helped. "The humans are starting to figure out how to use hydrogen fuels instead of oil based ones."

"Oh, how lovely." Yula clapped. "That's great. Oh, it would be a shame if the humans ran out of things to burn." She nodded sagely and set the glass down. "Such a shame.oh. Yes. So, two-thousand" She wiggled her fingers. "I think I was born, well, we're on our seventh generation. My great grandfather said he gave the humans fire, but he could have been lying. He probably just left it laying around somewhere and then," she threw her hands ceiling-ward dramatically, "-- whoosh. Suddenly the humans got it." She reached out her tiny hands for the drink and downed it gratefully. "Thank you, I was so thirsty."

Even Chloe looked at the empty glass as Yula returned to her, turning it in her hand as though it would melt.

"We've never had a salamander stay with us before." Barney had admiration in his voice for a change.

"Oh, well I I'm sorry to say but lately there's been some trouble at home." The redhead said sadly. "Our home was destroyed by human loggers. They're so barbaric and we had to scatter." Her head shook. "Violent creatures, I'll be glad when they finally learn some intelligence. I heard when they are born, they can't hold their heads up for a whole year." She turned back to Kana, staring wide eyed.

Kana, once again, was suddenly put on the spot. "Well I wouldn't say a whole year but, they do have bigger heads than they can carry."

"How odd." Yula exclaimed. "What about a bucket, to carry your head in?"

Kana's mind was reeling. She shook her head with increasing vigour.

"Okay, just stop. Everybody stop." She slammed her hands down on the leather couch. "What is going on here? We have a werewolf, a bloody vampire, some icy-touch person, and now little miss never-met-a-human. Can someone explain, please?"

"This is a refuge. Our Sanctuary." Chloe explained. Gabriella nodded. She was still lingering in the doorway to the hall; her back against the frame. "You heard Yula's story. She had to go looking for safety. We're it."

"Safety from what?"

"The loggers," Yula started, but Barney interrupted.

"Your kind," He snarled. "You humans are toxic. You pollute the world for the immortals who will remain when you die. You all make me sick. This house is refuge from your kind. And I cannot abide your staying here."

"We're not all like that." Kana hissed back at him. "Some of us actually care about the environment."

"Oh? And how do you help? Video games, movies, blindly and idly rotting away in your --"

"Barney." Gabriella warned. She stood upright, her back straight now. "Enough." The ice queen crackled her knuckles. Kana didn't blame her. Barney infuriated her too.

"So." Chloe said with enthusiasm. "What's a Salamander? What kind of fun things can you do? "

"Fire." Yula grinned. She turned to Kana, and spoke clearly, as if enunciating to a child. "You're old enough to understand fire right? It's burny, red like my hair, and it catches against everything. If you have something you don't want, I can show you."

"That's okay." Gabriella exclaimed, shaking her head and waved her hands frantically. "She knows what fire is. And por favor, I would not want you to burn down my house."

"Oh, it'll only take a second. In the hands of a professional, fire is quite safe." Yula grinned, laughing at Gabriella's worry. "Best kept out of children's hands, however."

"Agreed." Barney hissed. "Else it will make my job harder."

Kana felt that dig directed at her. She glared at him, only to be distracted by the weight of something jumping on her lap. Peering down, she gazed into the green eyes of a purring tortoise-shell feline. Gabriella had a cat?

Gabriella pulled a set of keys from her pocket. Kana pet the cat while it curled up on her lap. It purred contentedly, and head bumped her hand.

"Barney, would you like to show Yula the rooms? Let her pick one with a fireplace. We can incorporate the prices for the extra firewood into your bill. How will you be paying for your room?"

Kana wondered if she would be including fireproofing on that bill too.

"I have been selling blown glass on the side." Yula said quietly. "The humans have this thing they call an internet, and I send them pretty glass sculptures in the mail. It's fun and they give me their money for it."

"Cash in hand, cheque, or bank transfer?" Gabriella prompted, following as Barney led the Salamander girl up the set of stairs. The conversation faded out of earshot, so Kana focused on the cat, rubbing its belly when it rolled over. The tail flicked warily. Chloe plopped down into a vacant seat with a sigh.

"It's a quiet night outside," She said. "I'm tempted to go out and grab a bit of air. Getting pretty stuffy in here, no?"

"Yeah. Are you, " she hesitated, not sure how the blonde would take a joke. "Going out for a bite?" Kana's hand ran between the cat's ears, but she eyed the vampire warily. It would be so easy for her to do to Kana what she'd done to Gabriella earlier.

To her relief, Chloe laughed. "Nah, I don't bite humans anymore. Not if I can help it. Gabriella was an accident, and she understands that. I hope." Chloe almost looked wistful as she gazed over her shoulder out of the window.

"I guess when you heal that fast, that sort of thing can qualify as an accident" Kana said aloud, remembering Gabriella with the towel pressed against her shoulder. Much to her surprise, Chloe only laughed again.

"That's right. Damn, you know, you're really gonna have to watch yourself around here. You're pretty fragile, and Barney don't like you none. He isn't one to pull his punches, you know what I'm saying? Keep away from him, if you can."

"If you'd let me go home, please?"

"I can't. Honest injun, darlin', it ain't even my call anymore. Not only did you see me at the hospital, but now you've seen too much of this place."

"My Mum will go to the police."

"Well you best hope it don't come to that. Else you and your mama are both gonna be in a peck of trouble. No joke."

Kana didn't get the impression of a threat from Chloe, merely a warning. Bitterly, she peered down at the cat on her knee. It had stopped purring.

It let out a hiss, nipped her hand, and scampered off.

"Don't think she like you neither, *Chere*."

Kana sighed, watching the cat slink away. She really wanted to go home. Chloe seemed to notice her discomfort and offered her a melancholy smile.

"Hey, I bet a shower would cheer you up, no? You been in them clothes since you got here. C'mon, I'll lend you some of my clothes."

It wasn't the same as going home, but it did sound glorious.

"It won't be easy, with my leg."

"Oh yeah, I plumb forgot about that. You need help?"

"Well, no." Kana turned crimson. " I'll figure it out."

6

Kana paused, her tale as they rode on the train through India was interrupted by the wail and squirm of the restless child in her arms. He gave another soft whimper of noise, alerting her to his waking discomfort. She wrapped him tighter in the borrowed jacket, her own shoulders now bare without it, and affectionately kissed his cheek. At least the jacket would keep him warmer than she could.

"There now, Michael. Mama's here."

Theo's eyes remained fixed on Kana. She ignored the persistent stare, but was aware of it, although her focus remained predominantly on Michael. Clearly, the American man was bursting with questions but had patiently withheld them. Though still wary, she had opened up with increasing ease and as she told the story of how she came to live at Gabriella's Sanctuary, he hung on every word.

Kana brushed Michael's downy hair back from his face, his blue eyes opening slowly. She pressed her cold lips to his forehead. Michael squirmed, but now with an added giggle, clearly pleased at waking with a full belly. Even Theo smiled as a result.

"He has your eyes."

"Mm, he does. Has his Dad's nose though. Doubt he'll forgive him for that" Theo having never met the man, Kana knew he could neither agree nor disagree, but there was a clear difference between her own upturned button nose and Michael's crooked one.

"And his Dad's hair," She added, twirling a curl around her index finger. The difference between the fluffy, flyaway blond on the kid's head and Kana's own curly walnut brown shade was also obvious. Michael stretched, his tiny arms reaching up.

"You have questions?" Kana offered.

"Well, your Mom. "

"Yeah?" The brunette gave a tiny snort of laughter. Of all the things she had told him, he jumped straight to her Mother first?

"Well, she seems a bit distant."

"She was too involved in her work." Kana shrugged, seemingly indifferent towards the matter. "She liked our father plenty, but us… well, me, anyway… not as much. And given that I wasn't the easiest kid to look after, well, I can't say that helped much."

"Yeah," Theo looked away, peering toward a small huddle of women on the opposite side of the train carriage. Kana busied herself with the waking Michael. Bleary eyed, he was trying to figure out what was going on. Kana recognised the tiny pout.

"You okay, little guy?" She giggled again. Michael reached his hand out. Kana let him grab her finger and try to bite it with his gums while she waited for what she had told Theo to sink in. She found the confusion on his face amusing. It had been pretty much the same reaction she felt initially and to confuse someone else with it felt appropriate. It did wonders to improve her own mood.

"So when you said monsters?"

"I meant vampires, werewolves and pyromancers. And other exotic creatures besides." Kana gave him a matter-of-fact nod, her smirk only growing into a wide grin as Theo shot her a look of sheer bewilderment. She grinned. He could not have looked more flustered had she suddenly turned into a pumpkin.

"Look, lady, I like a good story as much as the next guy, but real monsters? You gotta be shittin' me." he rolled his eyes at her. His voice lost its cool for all of five seconds, Kana noted with an inward laugh. "So this Gabriella woman, she actually had ice growing from her hands over the werewolf dude? Like, real ice? Frozen water, ice?"

"Do you know of any other kind?" Kana persisted with her teasing. "I didn't believe it myself at the time, but it was definitely true. I'd been kidnapped by some ice queen and her pet vampire, but the others were more flamboyant in their supernatural gifts."

Michael wriggled in Kana's arms so she plopped him down on her lap, handing him a dummy from her bag to suckle on. No-one, to Kana's gratitude, seemed to be giving them the least bit of attention any more. Either they were oblivious or didn't speak English; she didn't care, so long as nothing came of it.

"So you think I'm making it up?" If he did, she wouldn't blame him.

"Aren't you?" Theo's eyes snapped to hers. "I don't mind if you are. You offered a story, and this is a pretty good one. But this is the real world. There's no such thing as real monsters. "

Kana sighed, a wistful smile on her face. She shook her head, her face the picture of sincerity. "Part of me wishes I could still believe that. Part of me is glad I know better now. Shall I go on?"

"We've still got plenty of time to kill. And like I said, it is a good story. Shaggy dog story, but I like it."

She burst into laughter at that. "Shaggy dog oh, that's good." Having someone to tell all this to felt wonderful; like lifting a burden. But before she could continue, the train dragged to a stop. Kana had no idea what station this was, but it wasn't hers; she wouldn't arrive at her destination until well past dawn.

Kana nor Theo moved; instead, they scooted further into the corner as they waited for sleepy, shambling passengers to disembark into the harsh orange floodlights of the platform. Those lights flickered across faces as some tried to depart while others tried to climb in; the knots of pungent humanity eventually disentangled, leaving the train carriage no less crowded than it was before.

A short, dark haired man with a cage stuffed with live chickens crouched beside Kana and asked questions in a language she didn't know; she shook her head in mute confusion. Michael pointed at the chickens in amazement. Theo chuckled but insisted Kana's point with; "No thank, pal. Keep walking, thanks."

"I give you one." He switched to English. "For you only three thousand rupees. Is good deal." He insisted, and Kana's foot slammed against the ground. Loud, hard and sudden, the lightbulb above them shattered with a pop and sprayed glass around them. Kana winced. That hadn't happened in a long time. She glanced around in panic and finally turned to the hawker.

"The answer is *no*." She growled at him, then leaned close and lowered her voice further. "I can make it even clearer, if I have to." Michael immediately burst into tears, and the man bowed low, scurrying off quickly. The entire carriage stared, wide eyed at her, while she soothed her child. Kana did not care and cuddled her child into her chest.

He had really wanted a chicken.

Theo was the only person on the train not staring at her, his attention solely focused on the crackling wires of the broken light up above.

"Sorry about that. Sometimes you really have to press a point." Kana grumbled, running her hand through her hair. Michael cooed and giggled once more.

"Yeah." Theo managed. "Well, that's what I call emphasis."

The storytelling paused as the pair waited for the staring to stop, and Kana waited for Theo's heartbeat to settle. Poor dear, she had really given him a scare. In fact, the whole carriage was wary of her sudden outburst. Except, of course, Michael. He always calmed down when he realised she could never focus her anger on him.

"So," Theo finally broke the silence. "This salamander girl, could she really set stuff on fire just with her mind? And was she all leathery and stuff, like the salamanders you find in ponds?"

"Yes, to your first question. No, to the second. She was cute as a button." Kana nodded, picking up Michael's spat out dummy and wet wiping it. "She was really skilled at making glass with it, just like she said. The house was full of glass work. Little tiny trinkets and glass animals, too." Kana shook her head. "She had her head in the clouds but, it was impossible not to like her. Hey, can you hold Michael a moment?" She insisted. "I'll be very quick, I just need to use the bathrooms. I trust you with him. Thanks." She plopped the child into his arms and fled before Theo could say a word.

"Wait," Theo blinked. Well, off went the girl, abandoning her child to him. Michael gurgled and stared through huge eyes at him. "Well, hello there. How you doing?"

Michael's big blue eyes blinked, still staring. For a moment, he wondered if Kana intended to leave him with the child, running away with his jacket, but she'd left her large diaper bag behind, along with the soup canteen. Surely, she would be back soon.

Theo didn't even know if this carriage featured a bathroom. The odds couldn't be very good. Michael curled tight against him. He couldn't believe quite how cold the kid was. "And who did you inherit that from, I wonder?"

Just as he was beginning to truly believe that she wouldn't return, the girl fluttered in through the doors at the end of the carriage. She was positively beaming. Theo tried not to show how relieved he felt. He held Michael out. Kana laughed and pulled him to her, rubbing her nose against his.

"Did you miss me, little guy?" She giggled. Michael's hand reached up to her face and tried to paw at her cheek, only making her laugh more. "He wasn't any fuss, was he?"

"Not at all. Did you find the bathrooms?" Her face had a rosier tinge to it and she'd dampened it with water. She looked much better. Maybe she simply needed some air.

"Mm," Kana replied noncommittally. "Where was I in my story?"

"The vampire just offered to lend you her clothes." Theo laughed. It sounded weird to say that out loud. Kana grinned.

"Chloe was a good friend in the end." She continued. " A really good friend. If not for her, chances are I wouldn't be here no, actually, I definitely wouldn't be here now." Kana sucked her lip under her teeth, settling back down beside Theo. He blanched, spying blood on her t-shirt. She had to be sick. Very sick.

"Are you ill?"

"What?"

"Are you ill? When you handed Michael to me, he was freezing, and you looked so pale."

"I'm fine." Kana replied more quickly. "Thanks, but I'm fine. Really. I am."

"Are you sure?"

"Leave it."

"Sorry, I don't mean to pry. I'm just worried for you and the boy, is all."

Kana sighed. "We've been traveling a while, and food's been difficult to find. Call it road fatigue, okay? Let's get back to the story."

Theo nodded slowly.

"Good." Kana shifted again. "Now, where was I?"

7

"You know while you're doing me favors, maybe you could think about taking me back home?" Kana gave the vampire a hopeful look as she sat down on Chloe's bed, draped in nothing but a large, fluffy, red towel. Being pampered with a gorgeous soak in a bubble bath in a stranger's house made her feel awkward. Sitting half naked in the tub with a cast on her leg that she had been instructed to absolutely not get wet, in any circumstances, was even more so. The two things together just didn't make sense. Even now, she still struggled to make sense of the whole vampire thing.

The arrangement of Chloe's room stretched out around Kana, identical to her own room with a double bed, wardrobe, chest of drawers and a bedside cabinet. Unlike her room, however, this one didn't have an extra door; no en-suite bathroom. Kana wondered if vampires even needed to use such things.

Chloe's face appeared from behind the open wardrobe doors.

Her hand followed after with a short purple dress, wrist thin at the hips, and held it up to Kana. The blonde's lips pursed, and both vampire and dress disappeared back into the confines of the wardrobe. Kana pressed the issue.

"I mean it's not like I could tell anyone the truth. Who in their right faculties would believe me? I could just tell my Mother I stayed at a friend's house."

"Maybe I'll just getcha some underwear first. You look about the same size as me." Chloe bustled away to her chest of drawers.

"My point is" Kana didn't want to push, but at the same time, the avoidance grated at her. "You are all completely safe. I don't want to cause any bother for you. I just want to go home, play some video games and have a nice, boring, mediocre life."

"Are you a B cup or a C cup? The difference between them seems to change, but the number bit confuses me." Chloe launched a few bras in Kana's direction. She didn't bother to catch them, letting the multi-coloured array of lingerie fall around her. She picked up a bright pink one and twirled the strap around her finger.

"All I want is to go home. Please." Kana repeated, her eyes on the floor. Chloe finally halted, a look of pity crossing her face.

"Kana," She spoke softly, leaning against the side of the dresser. "Darlin', I'm sorry. I wish I could let you, but you understand it's a matter of safety. Not just for us, Chere, for you, too. Even if you did get to go home, and you tried to keep quiet, your Momma might have already called the police. Damn sure she's gonna wonder why you ain't phoned. She's gonna wonder why you never took spare clothes. And what if the police have already contacted her? We were both on them cameras. What if the police think we was in cahoots? We've been lyin' low for so long, it's good this way."

"What difference does it make to me?" Kana finally snapped. Yes, she felt bad for Chloe, but this wasn't fair. "Why should I care what problems you have? You stole me on my goddamn birthday."

"Now, that's just your own fault, bein' stubborn. You wouldn't let go."

Kana paused with her mouth open. After a moment, she slowly closed it.

Chloe had a point.

"Whoever heard of a vampire stealing blood from a hospital, anyway." Kana muttered.

"Yeah it's in all the movies, vampires suckin' the blood out of folks." Chloe waved it off without even a smile. "But Gabriella thought it'd throw people off the scent a bit, rather than killing folks for their blood. I mean, if it weren't for that camera, I'd just have killed you straight out."

"You were going to kill me?" All colour abandoned Kana's face.

Chloe stared ominously for a moment before she nearly doubled over with laughter. "I'm teasin' you, darlin'. I don't want to kill anybody. That's why I went liftin' blood that was already out of the package, so to speak." Chloe grinned nervously. "You were just in the wrong place at the wrong time."

Oh great, Kana thought. "Well that makes it all a hundred times better." Her sour response was met by Chloe's hand on her shoulder. The girl jumped; hadn't she been at the other side of the room a second ago?

"I'll leave you some space to change, but, you know, I think you might even end up liking it here. Gabriella's cooking is pretty good too apparently." She laughed lightly. Kana could hear undercurrents in that laughter, though. Strain, a little envy, perhaps.

"My mum will come looking for me, y'know." Kana stared at the bra strap in her hand as she wound it idly around her finger. "The police will too. -"

"Yeah, that's the way I figure it." Chloe sighed. "Reckon we'll dynamite that bridge when we get to it."

The conversation grew stilted, so Chloe headed to the door. "Kana, we ain't bad people, okay? We might be a motley crew of creatures out of dreams 'n' nightmares, but we just want a normal life, as normal as life can be for folk like us, anyhow. Just take what you want from the closet."

When the door clicked shut, Kana let out her breath, sobbing slightly. She couldn't understand how she was supposed to feel sorry for these people. All the same, part of her did, As wild as the things they'd shown her had been, she knew Chloe was telling the truth.

She dressed as quickly as she could manage, into one of the bras and a pair of matching underwear, before settling on a cute red t-shirt from Chloe's wardrobe. Jeans were out of the question, but after hobbling slowly back to Chloe's bed, she slipped on a pair of black jogging bottoms easily enough.

An idea formed in her head.

This was a hotel, which meant they had a phone for bookings. Kana staggered to the doorway and yanked it open. Her leg ached angrily, but she tolerated it. Kana was grateful Chloe's bedroom was on the ground floor.

Never had she moved so quietly. Tentative footsteps made her rest weight on her right leg for far too long. Teeth grit hard together through the pain, she didn't utter a peep as she headed towards the living room. She was certain she remembered seeing a telephone in the corner of the room. Silence gripped the house, but Kana dared not question it, making her way slowly and steadily down the hall-way.

The grandfather clock in the living room ticked away to a slow beat. She could hear it already. Another faint clicking sound echoed with it. Gripping the frame of the living room door, Kana scanned the room.

The vampire had curled up on the couch in a dim pool of lamp-light. In her hands flicked a pair of knitting needles that met the tempo of the large clock. A thick line of pink wool led from the end of the needles down to the wooden floor where it zigzagged, and sloped back up onto the opposite chair. Kana's heart sank.

"That was quicker than a jackrabbit with a hound on his heels." Chloe smiled in her direction.

Kana frowned, fighting tears.

"Well, come on in," the vampire beckoned, crooking her needles under one arm to pat the seat beside her. "Sit y'self down."

Through the huge, partly drawn blinds of the large floor to ceiling windows, she could see that darkness had swallowed the sky. The grandfather clock proudly proclaimed eleven fifteen.

Despite the protest from her leg, Kana hobbled across the room to the furthest chair from Chloe before sprawling down into it. Her leg throbbed just below the knee where the fracture had occurred, and preventing her from standing back up. She needed to rest it; changing clothes had exhausted her.

"Mama taught me how to knit," Chloe returned to the rhythm of her needles. "Used to make them little figures, animals out of wool and crochet, then I would go sell 'em round the streets, back in Lou'siana. Every so often, mama would gimme a penny or something for candy. My reward for helping."

Kana shuffled, sitting up. She was curious where Chloe had come from. Her molasses thick accent and crazy clichés had been driving her mad with curiosity.

"Got a job somewhere we been keepin' you from?" Chloe's expression took on a shamed cast. "I hadn't thought of that. Money and the gettin' of it, I forget most times how important that is to regular folk."

"No. I'm just," she paused before admitting, "This place scares me."

"Oh." The needles clacked for a few seconds. "Guess I hadn't thought of that, either." The needles flashed and clicked. "I was seven when I started. Jobs were a funny thing back then. Hard to find, and not many people wanted to hire my Mama on account of her not having my Papa around."

Kana looked up. "What?"

"He left when I was a kid. He fell in love with the sound of a cork comin' out of a bottle. Every night, he'd go to the tavern to make that sound come to him. Well, one night, he just up and didn't come back. Kep' right on not comin' back from there."

Kana fought back a smile at the lyrical way Chloe told it.

"How did your mom…" Kana paused. It seemed too personal to ask how she died. After all, as a vampire, Chloe would have been around for centuries, giving her plenty of time to come to terms with it, unless Chloe's mother was a vampire too. "leave you? Or did she? I can't even guess your age, is she maybe still around?"

Chloe huffed a dry, mirthless bite of laughter. "Oh, she's long passed on now, darlin'. I reckon it were probably hunger in the end. Although I was already turned, by then. See, there was this voodoo queen, down on the bayou. Mama said I weren't to go down there, but hell, that old queen was fixed to pay a nice pile of scratch for a set of animals. Mama says no child, it'd bring down bad juju on us, dealin' with the hoodoo woman. Turned out more than a touch ironical, on account the old woman felt slighted by that."

Kana blinked. She'd only understood half of what Chloe had said, but enough to feel slightly disturbed. "Wait, she turned you into a vampire because you wouldn't sell her your crochet animals?"

"That's right."

Kana was wide eyed. Perhaps, with kidnapping, she'd managed to get off easily.

"I was seventeen." Chloe continued, eyes never having left the needles.

"That sucks."

Chloe raised her eyebrows.

"Sorry, I meant --"

Chloe loosed a thin trickle of laughter and focused solely on her knitting for a few minutes. The quiet ticking seemed obnoxiously loud through the otherwise still house. Even without the lights on, she could see the concentration in the vampire's evanescent blue eyes. The needles glinted.

The creak of the floorboards in the kitchen snapped Kana's head around so hard her neck cracked and she winced. Chloe instantly dropped needle and wool and jumped to her feet. In a flash of movement she leapt over the couch and covered the doorway.

"Lola?" Chloe asked, her head tilted curiously. "Y'alright Chere?"

There she was, blonde hair, dark eyes and bare feet. She seemed equally uncaring as to the mud of her feet and ankles as to the fact that she stood there naked. Kana tried not to stare, her face red. The kid looked like a cornered, wild animal.

At first, she didn't answer Chloe, opting only to shrug at the vampire.

"Where you been?"

"I was," For a second, the preteen seemed likely to talk, but after looking up and noticing Kana, she folded her arms over her chest and stormed out the other door, towards the hall. "I don't want to talk to her." Lola snapped, her voice just like her mother's. Apparently torn between banging her feet on the stairs in a tantrum, and trying to sneak up to her room, every third step became a hard slam of foot on flooring followed by the scuff of her feet trailing. The landing light upstairs clicked on.

Chloe and Kana shared a worried look.

"You think she's okay?"

"I think she's stepping over the threshold into puberty," growled an irate, and rather rough voice from behind. Kana turned to meet Vincent's eyes, and firmly set frown. Had he been following the girl? Stripping naked outside did not mean impending puberty to her; it screamed out for attention.

"You say that every time she does something you don't like." Chloe said, hand on hip.

Vincent favoured the vampire with a smirk, as though amused that he had managed to earn a rise from her.

" I don't think Lola likes me." Kana tried to convince herself she didn't care anyway.

"Women always find some reason to hate other women." Vincent said, shaking his head. Kana and Chloe both glared at him.

"Shush, listen. Gabriella's found her."

Chloe, Kana, and Vincent tiptoed to the bottom of the stairs and tilted their heads to listen. The sound of Gabriella's Spanish warmth had turned into a snarl of Spanish fury.

"But mum." Lola whined.

"No, Lola. You're out far too late and no clothes? I hope you changed inside the house. You are too old for this now. What if a human saw you?"

"Sorry."

Gabriella's sigh echoed down the stairs. "Come on, Lola. Let's get you ready for bed, si? At least you're safe. Where were you?"

"Playing up near the woods, I found a fox."

"Did you, now?"

Their voices faded out of Kana's hearing but the other two remained silent. Their hearing was obviously far better than hers.

"Eh. A skelped arse ought to have done it, too." Vincent finally shrugged and backed up into the living room to sprawl out over the nearest chair. "A yelpin' in the hall wouldn't sort nothing, anyway."

"That's a double negative." Kana muttered, feeling brave.

"A what, lass?" The wolf tilted his head.

"Never mind."

"Well, she got home safe, at least." Chloe said mildly, wringing her hands. She, too, retreated back to the living room and recollected her knitting.

"Aye, 'cause of me."

Kana hesitated at the foot of the stairs, considering finding a room to claim as her own, unsure if the one she had been deposited into counted as hers or not.

"I wouldn't." Vincent warned. "I'm guessing that shouting woke up just about everyone up there. You want to risk Barney yelling at you when you head up?"

The foot left the stairs.

"Come sleep here with us, Chere." Chloe offered. "We'll keep an eye on you."

Kana hesitated and shot her a look.

"Trust me, lass. If we wanted to maul you in your sleep, we've had an ocean of chances for it by now." Vincent chuckled.

Kana knew he was right. There had been plenty of chances to kill her already and the only one interested was Barney.

The wolf-man changed as he spoke, his bones crackled, he shucked his clothing, Kana quickly turned away, reconsidered it, and then turned to stare. Vincent became the same hulking grey mass of fur he had before. He shuffled towards the couch, and pounced on the vampire, knocking her to the floor.

"Vincent." She scolded. "You'll rip it. Careful." She raised her arms and pushed the beast away from her. He thumped to the ground and rolled over, itching his back in a shameless display against the floor.

Chloe rolled her eyes and gathered her knitting before Vincent coated it in hair. A grin tugged at the corners of Kana's mouth.

Vincent curled in the middle of the floor, and tilted his head at her. Now that she knew he did not intend to rip out her organs and feast on them, he didn't seem quite so intimidating.

The wolf whined. For some reason, perhaps pity, Kana felt obliged to kneel down and pet his head. More calm than before when he stopped her from leaving, she lowering herself down to the floor with difficulty and scratched his chin.

"Who's a good puppy?" Kana giggled, her voice twisted with humour. Vincent growled with pleasure, a meaty rumble that reverberated through the floor. Chloe shushed them both, but remained steadfastly focused on her knitting.

Damn, he was soft. Kana decided, and warm too. With a lazy yip, he pushed up close and buried his muzzle between her breasts.

"Bad dog." Kana hissed, feeling even braver than before. She tried to push him away but she had no more success that if she had attempted to shove a brick wall. He whuffled against her, refusing to move his face.

"Stupid mutt." She dared, and his tail thumped repeatedly against the floor. "Just behave, Vincent."

The sound of his thick tail thumping on the floor reassured.

The notion of falling asleep in the company of vampires and werewolves wasn't exactly conducive to slumber, but Kana managed. Despite their supposed natures, she felt surprisingly safe.

***

"Mum. I want to watch television. And she's still through there sleeping. Like, she's gonna sleep all day."

"She's a human, *hija*, what do you expect? Just go play outside while the sun still shines. Remember, humans heal in their sleep."

"Well she must be really broken. Nothing's happening. Her leg's still busted up."

"She is not broken, Lola. Humans heal slower than us. Don't be silly."

"Hmph. Not always. I saw on telly about this one girl who --"

"The same television that makes people like Chloe out to be ravenous monsters who can't behave themselves?"

A childlike huff. "Fine. But she's taking ages."

"It's only been a few days, Lola."

As Kana listened, half dozing on the couch, consciousness drifted in like a shallow wave.

It took several painful seconds to move, slowly inching her neck and head up and letting the bones crack audibly. Her body felt cold. When she'd dozed off, curled on the floor with the wolf wrapped around her, the heat had been suffocating but soothing. Now, wolf and vampire were gone, she was on the couch with a solitary blanket wrapped around her. She wiped sleep from her eyes with the heel of her palm, feeling her neck. No bite marks.

"Finally." Lola huffed, storming into the room and slamming her backside down on the carpet. Kana raked both hands through brunette curls, still trying to waken. The blare of some kid's programme assaulted her ears. Neither made any effort at conversation.

She flattened her fingers across the top of the couch, pulling herself up high enough to glance over the couch and through to the adjoining kitchen. Gabriella smiled over a mug of coffee.

"Morning. Well, afternoon now."

"Ungh," Kana replied, her voice raw with sleep.

"Breakfast?" Gabriella offered, finger directed at the white mug in her hand. Kana gave a slight nod. Finding her feet, she circled Lola, who swerved from side to side to see the television around Kana, and slowly hobbled into the kitchen.

Her leg itched and throbbed as Kana ventured into the kitchen. The room came into view. A back door led out into a moderated sized, closed off garden that she could partially see through the window above the sink and drying shelf. She eyed that backdoor hungrily.

"It's finished now." Lola complained. "I only saw the end."

Kana winced, hearing Lola from behind her. She didn't turn back, electing instead to continue her path to the wooden kitchen table.

Yula perched on one of the chairs, drinking from a large clear glass. From the colour of the liquid, Kana could safely guess it was more of Barney's whiskey. She tried not to look too overjoyed at his lack of presence, but only a little.

"Morning, human." Yula chirped cheerfully. Kana gave a small wave but immediately became distracted by the fluttering and clacking of something landing on the sink. Cackling and squawking, a large black crow now stood there, peering out from the sink, clattering its feet against the draining board.

They had a crow in the house. Right. Of course they did, why would they not.

Naturally, Kana's curiosity and fondness for animals rendered it impossible to ignore. "You have a crow?" She grinned, hobbling to the sink to watch the bird hop around. She reached out to stroke its little head. Unimpressed amber eyes stared back, but its grey beak opened lazily.

"Apparently, we do today." Gabriella chuckled. She busied herself with the kettle. "Tea or coffee?"

"Tea, please." It had not escaped the girl's attention that this woman had played accomplice in her abduction, and baffled her with her ice powers, but as long as they continued to play house, Kana would play along.

"Two sugars and milk, too. Please." Kana added as an afterthought. Gabriella nodded and turned to comply.

Once again, Kana's attention turned to the bird, watching those amber eyes as it tilted its head in return. "Hello, birdy."

Caw.

"So, you were saying that humans can eat meat *and* plants?" Yula asked Gabriella.

"I would not call myself strictly human, but *si*, we can. Omnivores."

"That's so *weird*. I should be writing all this down. I might struggle to remember it all."

"You're fine, Yula." Gabriella reassured her, now watching Kana and the crow. "Aren't you the same?"

"Well, not really." The salamander shook her head and pressed her finger to her mouth in thought. "We can eat meat, if we really have to, but we swore off the stuff a couple of thousand years ago. It seems uncivilised. Now, for our B vitamins we have a thing called soylen."

The crow cawed loudly in protest and Kana's hand pulled away reflexively to cover her face. The idea of losing an eye was not the least bit appealing.

"Kana," Gabriella chuckled, popping two slices of bread in the toaster and bumping down the handle. "Take a seat, rest that leg of yours and I'll make you some breakfast, Si?"

"Sure, thanks." Kana nodded, distracted. She still had one wary eye on the crow as she shuffled to the nearest chair and sank into it. It brought mild relief. Yula beamed at her from across the table and offered her glass. Kana shook her head. Whiskey was not her thing at the best of times, never mind five minutes after waking up. Even the smell threatened to sour her stomach.

"You should just chop the leg off," Yula suggested with a helpful beaming smile. "Quicker than waiting for it to heal up."

"What?" Every shade of colour drained from Kana's face.

"Yeah, just ssssnikt." The salamander gestured dramatically with her arms. "And a new one will grow in its place. If you need help cauterising the wound I can burn it for you." She nodded, matter of fact and clicked her fingers. A tiny spark flickered up from the red-head's hand. "No trouble at all, just a little blood."

"Human, Yula. Human." Gabriella shouted. "Do not burn or mutilate the humans. Their legs don't grow back."

"Oh, gosh. So flimsy. That's pretty inconvenient."

Kana felt suddenly nauseous.

"Si, but that's the way of it."

The crow gave another cackle and flew at Kana who screamed and covered her face, only to have the bird land on her arm and sidle up to her shoulder. It snapped its head this way and that trying to look Kana in the eye, but the brunette turned, hand covering the side of her face to avoid such things. It could still peck her eyes out and Kana had the feeling it wanted to.

"*Hija*, no flying in the *maldetta* house." Gabriella turned, snapping at the bird. Its head curled under a wing. Yula gave a tiny giggle. The toaster dinged, the newly heated bread scent fanning out through the room.

"Nice birdy," Kana muttered, free hand reaching up and around to pat the crow. It nipped her fingers and she yanked them away sharply, rather unnerved by having it sit on her shoulder.

"If she bites you," Gabriella warned, planting the tea and toast on the table before her, "just smack her off your shoulder." She emphasised her point with a sweep of her hand and a warning glare at the bird. As though in protest, the bird cawed and took off, fluttering down to the ground and bobbed out through the cat flap in the back door.

"Maybe she's upset because she missed her television programme." Yula offered.

"The crow?" Kana's face scrunched in her confusion. "Your crow watches telly?"

"Mhm. Far too much of it for my liking." Gabriella said, heading to the fridge to collect butter and some jams to put on the table beside Kana's tea and toast. "My daughter has a flair for melodramatics, particularly when she doesn't get her own way."

"That crow was Lola?" She leaned back to peer into the living room, craning her neck to look for the girl who had been watching the television at so loud a volume. If she was still in there, Kana couldn't see her.

"Si. She can shape shift."

"Oh, well, of course she can. Whatever was I thinking?" Kana mumbled. Had the cat been Lola too? She no longer felt hungry, but she took a tentative nibble. Gabriella smiled, nodded, and stood up.

"Yula, would you like anything to eat?"

"Do you have any chili peppers?" Yula clapped her hands together. Gabriella checked the fridge, pulling out a green bell pepper. She held it up. Yula gave a shrug, catching it as Gabriella threw it over.

As Kana picked at her toast, the room remained blessedly devoid of wildlife. Gabriella settled back into her chair to nurse her coffee, reading over a newspaper. The blare of the television continued to echo through into the kitchen, until suddenly; silence.

"Christ," That Welsh accent entered the room in the silence, followed by Vincent, who wandered in with his hands over his face. He stank of alcohol. He dropped the television remote on the kitchen worktop. "What time's it?"

"Nearly one." Gabriella said instantly, without looking at anything Kana recognized as a clock. "Why, what's wrong? Hair of the dog not working today?"

"I'm awake, s'what's wrong. How loud d'ye need a telly no-one's watching?" Vincent demanded, a scowl on his face at her pun.

"Well, perhaps you shouldn't drink so much, so late." Gabriella had yet to look away from her coffee. "At least you put Kana to bed at a reasonable time."

Kana frowned.

"Cork yer yap, wench." The grouchy blond werewolf shot at her before he slipped into the last remaining chair. "Urgh, what day's it again?"

"Tuesday." Again, Gabriella did not skip a beat.

Vincent grumbled. He hunched over the table, head in his hands and grunted.

"Grumpy perro" Gabriella grinned at Kana, who pursed her lips to hide the smile on her face.

"What's that, Gabby?"

"Nothing at all. Go back to your sulking." The Spanish woman waved him off as she stood and looked out the window. "It is sunny outside, I think I shall make the most of the weather and do some gardening." Gabriella stretched. "The flower beds at the end of the garden need de-weeded, anyone care to join me?"

"Can I burn the weeds away? I'll be really careful."

"No, Yula."

"Aww."

"You're alright, lass. I'll stay inside and wait for this to settle." Vincent gave Kana a nudge. "You couldn't rustle up me some eggs and bacon, could you? Settle my stomach."

Kana shimmied her chair to the side. She wouldn't give him the satisfaction of serving him breakfast.

Gabriella looked at him in disbelief. "She has a broken leg, Vince."

"Still?" Vincent, like the others, sounded annoyed.

"I don't know if you've noticed," Kana snapped, "But I'm a freaking human. I don't snap my fingers and magically grow another leg." Yula glanced at the floor, guiltily and Gabriella's eyes narrowed. "Hold on, let me just hop over on one leg.."

A low growl came from the hunched over wolf man. His head turned, watching her with bloodshot eyes, a thin bristle of blond hair on his curled upper lip.

"I've got a hangover, lass. If you're so squishy, maybe you shouldn't be yowlin' at a wolf with a migraine, eh? Now, fuck off, before I break Gabby's house rules."

"No. You fuck off."

"Kana," Gabriella warned, arms folding. Her backside pressed against the cupboard, watching the proceedings. "Do not wind up my guests. Vincent, stop badgering her."

Yula jumped to her feet. "Oh, I think I left something upstairs. I better go get it." She dove for the stairs.

Vincent had found his own feet. Looming over the girl with a growl, Gabriella's strength did nothing to pull the wolf man away from Kana's chair. Kana reached out to bat him away, but to no avail. She couldn't budge him. Her heart pounded in her throat as he snarled at her.

"You're lucky I like you, lass. You know why? Because one bite from me and I'd split your throat open. Let you gargle out a bloody river, and I bet the vampire would lap it up like slop to a pig." He leant in close enough for Kana to see the bloodshot veins in his eyes, and smell the alcohol on his breath. He shot her a wink, hidden out of Gabriella's vision. "I wouldn't mind eating the leftovers. Virgin meat always tasted fine to me."

"Vincent." Gabriella yelled. "Dios mío." She reached for a pan, ready and willing to make sure Kana wasn't hurt, and aimed it at him. But Vincent had yet to raise a hand. Instead, he took a step back and simply chuckled.

"If you need healin'," he added, "go talk to the vampire. I bet she could help. But stay the hell away from her teeth." He gave another bark of a laugh and sat back down. "Gabby, you found the pan. Well done, love. Make some eggs and bacon, eh? A man could starve in here."

Gabriella launched the pan at him anyway. He ducked, arm reaching up. The utencil hit his bicep and bounced with a deafening clatter.

"Christ, woman. What's your game? I was only having a bit of fun."

"You're not funny, Vincent."

"Bet I am, though."

Kana let out her breath, unsure what to make of him. She couldn't tell if he really had just been joking, or if he really did want to tear her throat out. Her hand reached up to her neck and held it carefully, swallowing.

Gabriella bent down to pick up the pan. Kana's eyes darted to the noise, but busily tucked herself with breakfast, relieved that Vincent's attention was no longer on her. She cradled the teacup in her hands, letting the heat console her. Vincent sauntered over to the bent over Gabriella, his hand came swinging around and smacked the woman across her backside.

Kana's mouth fell open.

The hand remained, squeezed, and a growl came from Gabriella, her hand tightening around the pan handle.

"*Cabrón*," The Spanish accent crackled from her. Kana could see the ice in the air. "You remove that before you lose it."

"Aw, love, come on. "

The woman swung around, the pan collided with jaw, and Vincent staggered, hand reaching up. Kana didn't move but couldn't stop a snort of laughter that burst from her mouth.

"Right, love." Vincent barked out an ominous laugh, setting the hair on the back of Kana's neck up on edge. He cracked his neck, tilting his head from left to right and launched himself at Gabriella.

Gabriella paused, then spun into a roundhouse kick. It reached up passed her broad hips and her booted heel collided with the exact same part of his chin that the pan had hit. Vincent snarled, and Gabriella's laugh trickled through the air like the gurgle of an icy stream. The wolf man now had a layer of bristling greying fur growing across his large arms and he grabbed the Spanish woman's arms, pulling her up and over the dishwasher, he slammed her head hard against it.

Kana's eyes darted between the pair. She drew in a sharp breath. Who did she shout for? So far when things went wrong she had yelled for Gabriella -- who was presently busy getting her head smacked against the kitchen. Should she yell for Chloe?

Before Kana could make up her mind, Gabriella seemed to shake off her dizziness long enough to kick back, her boots crunching down on Vincent's bare feet. He snarled, jumped back and Gabriella whirled around once more, blood dripping from a yellow gash across her forehead. The top of her thigh collided – hard – against the wolf man's crotch. His eyes bugged out as stumbled back and bent himself double across the opposing worktop.

"*Hijo de maladetta puta*." The Spanish woman screamed at him, and once again the pan clattered down against his skull. She slammed his head down in the sink forcefully enough for it to bounce. Vincent dropped to the floor like old meat, and Gabriella tucked a stray hair behind her ear as though there wasn't a gaping hole in the side of her head and a river pouring down her face.

"What. The. Hell." Kana finally blinked.

"What, you think he was in the right?"

"No, but you clocked him."

"Si."

A groan came from the heap on the floor, bristles gone, as he tried to find his feet.

"Fuck me, Gabby, you play rough these days."

"Keep your hands to yourself, *Carnero*."

"Psh. You're not even that pretty."

"Then why did you try to touch her arse?" Kana interjected. Gabriella smirked and raised an eyebrow in agreement. She, too, clearly wanted to know.

"Si, Vincent. Why?"

"Mount Everest, love."

Kana blinked. "What?"

"Never mind. I don't have to stay here and be abused by you women. I can find women anywhere who will gladly abuse me." Vincent hissed gruffly, wobbling towards the chair. "Least the hangover's gone. Just needed that healin' factor to kick in and wipe it out."

"*Bueno*. You can come help me buy groceries."

"Oh, let the heavens split open and ooze joy upon me."

"I swear you two are like a married couple." Kana exclaimed bursting into laughter. Though she had yet to see a married couple try to beat the living hell out of each other, it fit. Both Vincent and Gabriella looked at each other.

"No." They both said in unison.

Kana grinned.

8

With Kana's toast finally finished, Vincent settled with bacon and egg, and Gabriella slumped in a chair with a shard of conjured ice against her skull, peace finally suffused the kitchen. The only sounds in the room now were the delicate tick of Vincent's fork against his plate and the resounding tick of the grandfather clock from the nearby sitting room.

"Does this sort of thing happen often?" Kana asked. "The fighting, I mean." As long as they threw each other around without involving her, she would happily learn to accustom herself to it, from a distance.

Gabriella gave a tiny shrug. "Depends. A group of supernaturals under one roof, we get restless. We've lived this long together, what is another so many thousand years more." She shot a look at Vincent. "And some betas forget their place."

Vincent stuck his tongue out at Gabriella and continued to wolf

81

down his food.

Kana sipped her tea, choosing not to think about that last comment. She'd be lying if she said that she hadn't found Vincent and Gabriella laying into each other intimidating, but when all was said and done, the pair had calmed quickly enough afterwards with no hostility. It was like burning off stress, she realised. Perhaps even their version of horseplay. "Don't you ever break anything?"

"You break anything in Gabby's house," Vincent explained, "you run the gamble of bein' out on your arse. It's not a sure thing, but you're playin' odds."

"Si. And you still owe me for those sixteenth century Valencia vases you destroyed a few months ago. Or you will be too."

"Aye, I know, I --"

"-- when you stormed through drunk, and harping on about the --"

"I know, I know." Vincent insisted, covering his ears with his hands. "I can't heeear yooou. Lalalalalalala."

The shuffling of footsteps in the hallway alerted Kana to another presence and silenced Vincent. With so many bodies wandering around in such a busy bed-and-breakfast, there couldn't be much time for sitting around, especially for Gabriella.

"It's a bit early for clownishness, isn't it?" The sour baritone of Barney hit Kana's ear. She frowned in reflex. "Are you two so hard up for entertainment you need to wake the entire house? What about your new pet?" He chuckled to himself and Kana's frown deepened. She glared at him.

Vincent patted her shoulder before using her as leverage to stand. He made a show of giving Barney a ridiculously large berth on his way to the fridge to grab the finale to his breakfast. A finale which consisted of a bottle of alcohol; this time chilled.

"Hair o' the dog. Ha." He chuckled to himself as he slammed back down into the chair and took the cap off with his teeth. Kana winced watching him.

She wrinkled her nose in response to the overpowering vanilla-and-licorice scent of rum. Drinking first thing in the morning was something her Mother would have had words about. From the casual manner in which Gabriella took Kana's breakfast plate and popped it into the dishwasher, the alcohol didn't even appear to be a blip on her radar.

"It ain't like the stuff we used to have," Vincent said with a disconcerted sigh, "but it gets the job done."

"Si," Gabriella chirped, a nostalgic smile piercing the faraway looking in her amber eyes. "The rum these days does not have quite the same fire. I wonder if we should try making our own again."

"Aye, well I did have a knack for it."

"You?" Gabriella quirked a brow.

Kana's eyes bugged. "Isn't that illegal?"

Gabriella and Vincent shared a long look before bursting into raucous laughter. Barney rolled his eyes so hard it looked painful. He pulled those leather gloves of his tighter up his wrists.

"Aye, lass," Vincent chuckled, hand not clinging to the drink jostling her shoulder. "S'illegal, and you don't want to be getting yourself mixed up in illegal stuff, you could" he broke down into raucous laughter again, clearly unable to finish his sentence. Gabriella fought hard to keep her own laughter to a minimum. Kana remained confused.

"I don't get it." She muttered.

"Pot, kettle, black, Kana." Gabriella's shoulders shook with mirth. "Pot, kettle, black. Vincent can't even say it with a straight face."

"No one is fighting anymore, are they?" Yula's voice squeaked from the doorway. She wrung her hands together, huddling up in the corner of the hallway, peering in, looking like some victim of a great tragedy. Barney shook his head and beckoned her in.

"No one would dare while I'm here," he said, a proper smile finally creasing his gaunt cheeks.

"Hah." Gabriella concluded, raising her coffee once more and burying her grin behind it, mirth still visible in her eyes. Yula awkwardly returned Barney's smile before waltzing back in and Barney was quick to offer her his seat. Gabriella quirked a brow, but said nothing. Vincent wrapped his lips around his bottle and drank deep once more, clearly ignoring Barney. Kana couldn't help but be impressed at his skill at it.

Though Vincent's words caused equal irritation to Kana as Barney did, she couldn't decide who annoyed her most. Although Vincent, to his credit, despite having knocked her over, never caused a bruise like the purple eyesore that still ringed her wrist. Yula plopped down into the seat she had abandoned and curled up. Bare feet pressed flat against the seat, her head resting on her knees. From the glare of the afternoon sun through the kitchen window, Yula's flaming red hair looked on fire. Vincent stared at it intently, and Gabriella's glance noticed it. The salamander herself was oblivious, only noticing her hair when a stray lock of it fell into her eyes. She blew it back carelessly and tucked it behind her ear.

Barney's image remained lost in it till her fingers swiped the short strands back when he turned and stalked to the fridge, burying himself in it. Kana continued to stare.

"Here lass," Vincent finally broke the silence, bottle now emptied. "Could you chuck this in the bucket?" He held the bottle out and waggled it with one finger stuck inside the neck.

"Me?" Kana asked, but before she could agree, protest, or even attempt to stand up, Gabriella was behind him, grabbing the bottle and yanking it from his finger with a wet pop. With a sigh, she headed to the back door, opened it and headed out to the bins behind the house.

"Cerdo perezoso." She teased, her voice half obscured by the clatter of glass hitting the bottom of the appropriate bin. Kana craned her neck again, trying to take in a better view of the garden while Vincent chuckled to himself.

"What did she say?" Kana asked.

"She said I'm a lazy pig." He grunted, sinking lower into the chair.

Well, she's half right. Kana decided inwardly, pulling a disgusted face.

"Si." Gabriella nodded, re-entering the house and stretching as she closed the door. "Cerdo perezoso. Keep it in your mind, Kana. You will need it living here."

Kana gave a nod, though she did not anticipate ever using it on someone who could bite her head off, should the fancy strike him. His mood swing earlier, playful or not, had unsettled her. Punching him hadn't exactly been planned though and yet she still lived. That said, Chloe had proven to be a good person. She hoped Vincent would turn out to be okay too. She eyed him warily.

"Costs five quid to stare, love." He smirked. Kana resisted telling him where to go. Barely. She cast her eyes away, looking towards Barney and Yula. Barney had usurped Gabriella's chair and the pair were huddled close, fully engrossed in a conversation too quiet for her to hear. Every few words, Yula burst into giggles, and nodded, her finger reaching up to her mouth to nibble on the nail. After a few seconds, she reached out her hand and took Barney's glove, trying to pull it off.

Kana had never seen anyone move so fast. Gabriella let out a yelping scream and launched past Vincent and Kana toward Barney. Yula squeaked, eyes wide and scrambled behind Vincent.

Gabriella and Barney flew backwards, clattering into the cupboards.

Kana froze.

Her eyes landed on Gabriella's arm. Reaching out to catch herself, her forearm had collided with Barney's bare jaw. Kana might not have registered it as note worthy; if not for what happened next.

Barney hissed, head smacking the cupboard door, but Gabriella sank to the floor like a broken doll, limbs loose, and her pupils dilated. Vincent rolled his eyes, strolling to the fridge for another bottle of alcohol. Kana swallowed, fighting the urge to scream, and Yula covered her mouth with her hands, visibly shaking.

Barney was the first to rise. He grabbed Gabriella by the scruff of her collar and flung her limp body toward the sink before staggering to his feet. He groaned, brushed himself off, and his gaze shot to Yula.

"Stupid woman. "

Barney had killed Gabriella just from the touch of bare skin.

"What the fuck are you?" Kana shouted. Yula continued to violently shake, wringing her hands. Kana watched the redhead. Unable to stop, the tiny girl let out a whimper and burst into flames.

"Holy, " Kana scrambled awkward to her feet and knocked the chair over. She fell back, crashing against the floor. Her head thumped against the immediate wall, enough to blind her. She whimpered, an aching throb coursing through her head and up her leg. Her head spun.

Gabriella was lying limp on the ground and Barney had killed her by touching her. Yula was on fire and the surrounding kitchen was catching. Kana's head pulsed.

"Jesus." raced out the back door like a shot from a gun. Kana whined. *Coward.* He could have taken her with him. She groaned, her hand feeling at her head. Fuzzily, she peered at her fingers.

Red. Bleeding? Wait, wasn't there something more important going on?

Her hazy gaze dragged back toward the inferno swirling around the kitchen. Barney had backed up to the edge of the kitchen, watching as fire licked the ceiling. Kana backed up on her hands and backside, trying to reach an exit. Her leg weighed her down.

She dared not go closer to Barney. That left the entrance to the living room as the only possible exit; the flames had already reached the back door and were blackening the wood

As she shuffled away, the smoke clutched at her lungs only making the world spin around her. Moving her arm across her face, she moved, only partly aware that, should she reach the front door, she couldn't reach up for the handle.

The heat of the flames washed over her skin in waves. Not close enough yet to burn, but enough to grip and pull her senses. Only partly aware of the wet trickle down the back of her neck, she stopped as her back hit another kitchen counter. The air tasted of wood and ash; it burned her lungs with each gasping breath. Scrunching her eyes, she tried to force away the smoke and shake off the disorientation. The flames danced around her. Creeping closer, they now lapped hungrily at the kitchen table and charred the cupboards.

"Enough. *Madre de Dio.*" Gabriella's fury rang through the roar of the flames. Kana was only partially aware of her storming furiously into the blazing kitchen. Her voice carried louder than the fire and she saw the kitchen slowly frosted over.

Snapping and popping, the ice rippled through the room as the frost and the fire fought for dominance. Even now, Barney had not moved, watching everything through the hallway entrance as though either helpless or entirely nonchalant.

"Yula." Gabriella insisted through gritted teeth. Whatever force was freezing the kitchen over was working as the black smoke surrendered to a blinding fog bank of steam. Kana stared blankly at the pair, half choking.

"You need to control this. Stop burning my house." Gabriella soothed her. The floor crystallised; shiny, wet and frozen. The water taps imploded, ripped apart by the rapid contraction of the water within them. The ice spread up the cupboards. Finally, Gabriella reached Yula's flaming body. She pulled her into a move that was a cross between an embrace and a choke hold.

"It's okay. Hush now calm, "Gabriella's icy tones spread across the room.

The fire stopped. The salamander was sobbing. Finally, the pangs of nausea and darkness tugged Kana under against her will.

***

"More. You need to drink more, Chere."

Kana protested with a hoarse moan in the darkness. Arms pushed out, trying to force the insistent pressure from her mouth. It held fast and she wriggled, but a throb stabbed the back of her skull. With consciousness came more pain that pulsed and slowly ebbed away from her leg. She winced, groaned and tried to pry her eyes open. Purple spots faded into vision.

Chloe peered down with worry etched into her soft features. The smoke charred features of Gabriella's kitchen burred in Kana's vision, wavered, before coming into clarity. Had it been a nightmare? No; the soggy blackened remains of wooden cupboards, cracked ceramic worktops and a splintered sink meant it had been all too real. Kana sat with her back against a wall, in a puddle of melted ice. Her teeth clacked, and she peered up at Chloe.

From the other room, Gabriella's frenzied tones burst into her earshot.

"You could have grabbed me, or at least her, and pulled her out of the kitchen door, outside, to safety."

"I was tryin' to get your garden hose, you stupid wench. Get off me."

"You broke my *maldito* shed." Gabriella snarled back.

"Because I was in a *hurry* to get your garden hose."

The rage descended into a tirade of furious Spanish that Kana couldn't keep up with. In the living room, she could see and hear Yula and Barney. The pyromancer was sobbing, her tiny body curled into Barney's leather jacket. He stroked her fondly through his leather gloves. She could see the tentative quality in his movements.

"I'm sorry. I'm sorry. I didn't mean for it to happen. I didn't mean for it to happen." The tiny woman sobbed.

"It's all right." Barney hushed her. "No-one was hurt." Kana didn't miss the disappointment in his tone. "No-one was hurt or killed, and you didn't mean it."

The voices were chaotic, causing a riot of noise in the house.

"Cabrón. My shed is broken, and you still didn't bring the hose."

"Yula, please don't cry. No-one is blaming you."

"Ah, you're a miserable wench. You can get it fixed easily. Hell, I'll fix it."

"I thought she was dead for real, Barney."

"You're not touching my shed again."

Yula had literally combusted. Gabriella had been killed by Barney's bare touch and then stood back up again. Lola was a crow. And yet, the only thing Kana could think about was, "I'm not supposed to get my cast wet."

Chloe gave a wry chuckle and nodded. She lifted her arm up, and Kana dry retched at the sight of the deep gash torn in the flesh. The vampire had been holding the sides open, trying to get Kana to drink. But she recoiled at the sight the viscous blood. It was almost like a maroon tar, as it oozed from the wound. It did not drip, as though desperate not to part from her flesh.

"Kana, do you think you can drink a lil' more? Your head is still bleeding real bad. This ought to help you out some."

More? Kana felt pressure in her stomach and the back of her throat. Vampire or not, the idea of drinking Chloe's blood was not only ludicrous, but because of how sickened she felt by the sight of the wound, it was damned near impossible. Kana lifted her hand up to her lips. Moisture clung to them. When her fingers came away laced with the maroon substance, her insides tightened. Deep down, she knew Chloe was trying to help, but that didn't make it any easier. Nor did the smell. The scent of rot attended the liquid, adding to the repulsion.

"Drink," Chloe urged. "I can't hold my arm open all day. It wants to heal."

"No, I can't."

"Dammit, girl." With the strength of an eighteen wheeler truck, Chloe grabbed the back of Kana's head and slammed her face against the open wound. She stiffened, squealed, and held her breath. The vampire persisted. Finally Kana's protests stopped. The other house guests were far too preoccupied to help her, and thus Kana was forced to submit and breathe in the ghastly smell.

"Drink." Drinking wasn't quite the word; the substance too thick, like dried glue, and it stuck to the sides of her mouth on the way down. All the while her body fought, as though it knew this unnatural substance was not meant for human consumption. It had a vile acrid taste, like soured meat best left to flies and carrion birds. Her eyes watered, but Kana forced it down.

"Attagirl." Chloe's attempt at reassurance did little for her. Kana coughed violently and retched hard, her body jerking forward from the very second the vampire's arm moved away. Her stomach knotted.

The effect was instantaneous. With a sudden rush Kana's blood began to pound through her body with increased vigour. Her dizziness increased with it, head lolling back against the wall. Vision blurred to a gauzy blend of yellows, purples, and reds before settling into a world more vivid than before. Everything looked vibrant and sharp, as though the contrast of reality was normally hazy and suddenly turned on full power.

She could hear the melody in Yula's tears, the purr in Gabriella's voice; hell, she could hear the howl in Vincent's biting retorts. Kana peered at her hands. With crystal clarity she could see the skin almost glowing. Turning to Chloe, she noticed a visible difference. Chloe's skin lacked that same lustre, the same illuminating glow. By instinct, she knew it meant the vampire was dead and she was not. So she hadn't been turned then, merely 'improved'.

"Whoa," Kana gaped and Chloe's laughter rang like bells, the sweet cadence of her voice akin to a symphony of tiny violins, and yet at the same time it sounded like layers of glass running over each other. Kana couldn't settle. "Is this what being high is like?"

"I have no idea, Chere." Chloe grinned, her eyes like brilliant diamonds of blue. "Vampires don't get no effects from that. Least, I don't. Here, let me get you some water." She stood and headed to the sink, before pausing, realising the state of the sink.

"Oh well, or not."

It was Kana's turn to laugh.

The whole situation was ghastly, but the look of confusion on Chloe's face when she turned around to face her, realising the faucets had exploded, broke all the awkwardness left in the room.

Gabriella and Vincent had stopped arguing. She could hear Gabriella ranting on the phone to her insurance company with the occasional Spanish word flying out accidentally in her rage, and who could blame her? Her kitchen had been charred and blackened. What hadn't burned was soaked, the remaining puddles evidence of that.

She could hear Vincent's every footfall as he slowly walked into the kitchen.

"Bloody woman's wired to the moon." Vincent grumbled and shook his head. He finally noticed Kana. "Christ, lass, your pupils are like saucers. What've you been doing now?"

"I gave her some of my blood. Think bein' a vampire will suit her, Vincent?" Chloe teased.

It worked. He scowled, knelt down to a crouch, and peered closer at Kana, tilting her head for a better look at her skull. He pressed fingers to her scalp. Even his scent was heightened by the vampire's blood flooding her senses. Strong and boozy, a little salty with a hint of licorice. Is this what the world was like to Chloe all the time?

"No." Vincent snapped, a delayed answer to Chloe's question. "She's better off as a human." He grabbed for Kana's leg. She screamed on impulse.

"*Dios mio,* What now?" Gabriella hollered, though still on the phone, couldn't leave her post.

"Nothin'. Clog yer howl hole, wench." Vincent hissed. "Kana, ain't it?"

Of course he knew her name. Everyone in the house did, some from malice, others from pure curiosity. Kana had the strongest urge to kick him with her other foot, but that was stupid. She tensed instead, glaring at him.

"Don't even try it, girlie."

"Oh God. Don't tell me you're a mind reader, too." She just knew that one of them would be. Of course it would be the most arrogant one in the bunch.

Chloe rolled her eyes but Vincent grinned, smug.

"Instincts, love. Instincts. Simmer down, and relax your leg. Go'an. Let it go limp. I won't hurt ye'. Just trust me."

Kana frowned. She didn't trust him in the slightest, but she did as he asked, releasing enough tension in her leg that he now held it up with his arm. She prayed he wouldn't drop it, even accidentally.

"Ready?"

"For what?"

He brought his clenched fist down hard, slamming it with tremendous force into the cast. Kana felt the rattle run all the way up her body. She winced, expecting pain, but none came. The cast shattered around her adding to the disorder of the kitchen. Vincent grinned and politely pulled down the bunched up pant leg of Chloe's borrowed tracksuit bottoms, sliding the black material over Kana's leg. It was sweet and very unlike the annoying version of Vincent. He patted it in satisfaction and set her bent knee down to the floor so her foot was ready to hold weight, reaching out for her hand to help her up.

"You might want to thank Chloe for gouging her arm open for you." He nodded sideways, in the direction of the vampire. "Creepy as they are, their blood's pretty potent."

"My leg's fixed?." Kana gasped, only half aware of being pulled to her feet. "Wow, that is so cool. It doesn't hurt at all. "

Chloe positively beamed. "The effect of the blood is indiscriminate, Chere. It just goes where it wants and mends what needs mended. Also, you're welcome."

Kana nodded, her thank you unspoken but unnecessary. As she found her feet, the swing of the cat flap revealed a large brown rat that scampered into the house and scurried past Kana's feet.

"Please tell me that was Lola." She cringed.

"Aye." Vincent chuckled heartily.

The rat turned, metamorphosing into a tall blonde and automatically, with his gaze averted to Lola's nakedness, Vincent swiftly tugged his own shirt over his blonde head and it to the shapeshifter. She popped it on, wearing it on her skinny frame like a tent.

"Mum." She scrambled through into the living room. Kana walked without pain towards the doorway and peered in. "Mum. One of the neighbours kids is watching the "*Amazing Mary-Sue.*" at his house. He has the plus one channels and his bedroom window is wide open. Please can I go visit him? I promise not to turn human around him and stay a crow at all times. I won't even go inside, I'll just stay on the window ledge real quiet."

Gabriella placed her hand over the mouth piece of the phone and shoo-ed her off with a nod. Lola squeaked happily, shrunk down into a rat again and wriggled free of the t-shirt, leaving in on the floor, as she clambered back out of the cat flap.

Kana blinked, looking at the other two.

"Did she just,?" She didn't finish her sentence. Either Lola, in her haste, hadn't noticed the destroyed kitchen, or this kind of situation happened far too often for her to care.

9

The doorbell rang early, waking Kana with a start. The sound of bells echoed through the entire house and for a blurry moment, she couldn't be sure if she had been dosed with Chloe's blood again.

As reason found her, so did a sense of disappointment in herself. She had intended to sneak off during the night and waking up to the sun behind the curtains only left her feeling even more trapped. She swore inwardly.

However, whoever was ringing the doorbell was a more pressing matter. Forgetting her newly recovered leg, she sat up. She grinned as memory, and lack of pain. She could walk again. Chloe's pale pink pyjamas fit just as well as her own did, but she readjusted the bottoms, which had shifted in her sleep.

The best sleep I've had in days, Kana mused.

She tiptoed across the room, the creak of the hotel's front door alerting her. Opening the door by the tiniest inch, Kana pressed her eye to the gap, eager to see who the newest house-mate would be.

"Hola? How can I be of service?" Gabriella's voice sounded almost amicable.

"Good morning. We are looking for Gabriella Montigo, the owner of this establishment." A stern male voice echoed through the hall.

"Speaking."

"Is my daughter in there? I want to see my daughter."

"Please, Ms Lindqvist."

"I want to see my daughter."

"Would you like to come inside?" Gabriella offered.

Kana gasped with shock. Her mother had found her. which meant she had actually taken time away from work to come looking.

"Yes, that would be best, thank you."

"We would like to ask a few questions." The male voice insisted as several pairs of footsteps trampled into the bed and breakfast. Kana could see Gabriella, the flash of police uniform, and the shape of her mother disappear into the living room. She could run out right now, and she'd be free.

Unless Gabriella killed them. Kana remembered Gabriella's words back in the Mercedes. The Spanish woman hadn't been adverse to Chloe just outright killing her and there were no security cameras here. Kana would have to plan this carefully; as strained as things could get, it wasn't as though she could stand to get her mother flash frozen, to say nothing of the other improbable fates this place held in store.

The voices continued in the living room, and Kana had a feeling everyone in the entire hotel could hear. "Ms. Montigo, are you aware your Mercedes was seen at the General Hospital several days ago? Can you remember why that was?"

"Oh." Gabriella sounded pensive. "Are you certain it was my car?"

Another female voice rattled off the car's license number. The door creaked as Kana leaned against it.

"I've had enough of this. We all know my daughter is in here. Enough." Karol's voice rang out with impatience. "Kana." She shouted out.

"Ms Lindqvist, would you prefer to wait outside?" The female voice grew cold.

"No. I want to find my daughter."

"Then please calm yourself."

Kana nibbled her lips. Her mother's current mood did not set her at ease. If she were to head out now, Kana had a feeling her mother would blame her.

"Ms Montigo," Luckily the male voice redirected the conversation. "Would you kindly tell us why you were at the General Hospital? Before you answer that, I should advise you that we have the footage from the hospital's closed circuit cameras. Please note that anything you say can be used in court."

Guilt flooded Kana's senses. Gabriella could not go to prison, she had a hotel to run: a vampire, a werewolf, a Barney, a salamander, and a daughter to look after. There could be no telling where they would go if she was incarcerated. Not to mention, with her ice skills, it seemed unlikely they'd ever get her to go quietly. More violence would help no one.

She yanked open the bedroom door and scrambled through the house, winding to a halt at the threshold to the living room.

"Wait." She exclaimed. "Gabriella was picking me up."

She took in the sight in the living room. Gabriella calmly sipped her morning coffee, two police officers, one man and one woman, sat on the couch with her mother bracketed between them. Karol's eyes widened.

"Kana." She exclaimed, breaking free of the officers and running to hug her daughter. She pulled the girl into a bone crushing hug.

"Ack." Kana winced. "Hi, mum."

"Kana," Her mother held her at arm's length and looked her up and down. "Do you have any idea how worried I was? How dare you not phone? What happened to your leg? Where is your cast? Did you make the Doctor cast an unbroken leg just to spite me?"

Kana was too shocked and disappointed to speak.

"I knew it wasn't a break." Her mother raged, "I swear Kana, this had better have been some game just so you could go out and get drunk on your birthday. I had to phone the police. You've made me look stupid in front of everyone. Are you proud of yourself?"

The police officers stood, looking awkward. Gabriella's eyebrows narrowed and she sat forward, but all she did was sip her coffee with barely restrained contempt.

"Miss Lindqvist. Kana. " The female officer interrupted her mother's rant. "May we ask you some questions?"

"Oh, I have questions." Karol hissed, fuming. Her jaw had set and she had a firm grip on Kana's shoulder. "I am so disappointed in you, Kana. I told you, home by ten. Instead I had to go through the police. Do you know the danger you could have been in?" She pulled her daughter into another hug but it felt false, only a show for everyone looking..

Kana tugged free and shot her mother a look. So much for her mother being worried, *worried for her image more like*. Her eyes prickled. She felt stupid for thinking her mother might just be grateful to have her back.

"Just you wait till we get home, young lady."

"I'm not going home."

Kana firmly declared, folding her arms. She didn't realise she meant it until the words were already out. She did mean it. Karol's attitude had reminded her of just how much she disliked it at home. Here, it felt almost better than home.

"Excuse me?" Karol's eyes were wide enough to cause alarm. She reached for her daughter. "You will do as you are told."

"Probably not," Kana stepped back out of reach. "I'm staying here with Gabriella. I texted her to pick me up and she, her daughter, and her family have been looking after me and letting me stay here."

"Kana if you think I am going to pay to let you stay here then you have another thing coming-"

"Ms Lindqvist." Gabriella's smile was manic as the woman stood up and placed her coffee cup on the corner table's coaster. She laced her fingers together. "Kana is happy here, and I am allowing her to stay here. She is welcome to stay as long as she likes. I don't think I will have people threatening my guests. I suggest that you leave. It does not look as though calling the police is necessary." She tilted her head and raised her brows in a barely concealed threat.

If Karol could breathe fire, she would have done so.

"Kana, you get in that car right now." She ordered, pointing at the front door. "You are my daughter and you will do as you are told."

"Actually,"The male police officer argued, "Your daughter turned nineteen. She is now legally able to make her own decisions. If she wishes to remain here, it is well within her legal rights."

Gabriella did not bother to hide her smirk. Kana found her own smirk tugging the corner of her mouth. Somehow, this just felt right.

"Alright, Kana." Karol said, taking a deep breath. "You do as you wish. But if that's the case, you will come home and collect your things. I'll not have your shit in my fucking house if you're not even living there." The woman huffed, and then stormed out the front door, slamming it hard enough to rattle.

"I'm sorry." Kana cringed.

Gabriella walked over, put an arm around her shoulder, pulling her close.

"I can supply you with change of address forms, Kana. It will take some time, but we can help you." The female officer advised. "Are you happy with this, Ms Montigo?"

"Of course, Officer. We are more than happy to have her." Gabriella smiled warmly in Kana's direction. "She's already quite like a daughter to me."

Kana blinked back the burn of tears and peered up, seeing true kindness in Gabriella's eyes. The tears slowly slid down her cheeks. Embarrassed, she wiped her eyes with her palm. Gabriella squeezed her shoulder gently, reassuringly.

Kana took a deep breath. If she so wished it, she might never see her mother again. She found melancholy at that; but at the same time, relief.

"Thank you, Kana."

She felt confused. Gabriella had the softest look on her face that Kana had ever seen on anyone. The ice woman looked warm and huggable.

"For what?"

"I'll explain later."

Kana smiled, still wiping her eyes. "Thanks, Gabriella. For everything. Especially for giving me a good home. I really needed one."

Now Gabriella looked ready to cry. She didn't of course.

Ice queens were too tough for that.

"Well,"The male officer cleared his throat in the midst of all the emotion. "There is still one other thing we need to address, regarding your companion."

"My companion?" Gabriella turned towards the police officers now. "What companion?"

"The blonde girl in the hooded jumper. Again, our security camera footage tells us she entered the car."

Gabriella's finger moved to her lip.

"Oh, I think I know who you mean. Kana, would you be so kind as to go knock on door one-zero-seven on the first floor?" Gabriella enunciated clearly.

"Sure." Kana wondered what Gabriella had planned. Still puzzled, she walked past the stairs and knocked on the door seventh in the hallway; the last room on the first floor. It opened slowly, and Chloe stood behind it with a grin.

"Hey, we have a problem."

Chloe pressed a finger to her lips and beckoned Kana inside. The door shut firmly, and only then did Chloe speak.

"Well, what do you think? I have never tried being another person before. Did I get it right? Did I?" Chloe bounced up and down.

A carbon copy of Chloe sat on the bed with folded arms and a pleased look on her face. " Right smart trick, ain't it, Kana?"

Realisation hit. "You're Lola." Kana gasped.

"Yup."

"Remember the plan, Lola?" Chloe said quietly. "You hustle yo'butt all the way to Calais just as fast as you can before you head back, alright? Make sure they see you headin' that way, make sure they chase you, but don't get caught."

"I know, I know."

"Wait," Kana interrupted. "She's going to lure the police away? But she's just a kid."

"I can totally do this, darrrlin'." Chloe's doppelgänger announced, haughtily drawing out the last word in imitation of Chloe's drawl. "You're just jealous 'cuz I'm special."

"No, I love that you are special. Lola, you can be a cat and climb into my lap anytime you want. I love animals. Although, the crow did scare me." That earned a chuckle from the feisty shape-shifter. "But this is big trouble. I'm worried for you." Kana shook her head.

"It seems dangerous."

"Pfft. It'll be so easy."

Kana threw a worried look at the Chloe on the bed. She nodded.

"Okay, well. Right. Guess you'd better come downstairs with me then, Chloe. They're waiting for you."

The girl masquerading as Chloe grinned and nodded, excited to be playing this game. She followed Kana back down the stairs.

"Gabriella," Kana said, trying her best lying voice. "Was this the girl you meant?"

Chloe Mk II appeared in the doorway.

"Ah, yes." Gabriella said. "I don't think I took a note of your name, Miss. What was it, again? You've been here since Thursday, but we've barely seen you at supper."

The police officers rose.

"Sandra-bella Montrosoi, of course." The blonde replied, mincing in the doorway. She pushed her hair behind her ears and Gabriella, who had retrieved her coffee, snorted into it. "What can I do for you police type people?"

"We have a few questions you might be good enough to help us with."

Kana noted that Gabriella gave Lola the tiniest of winks, just out of the officer's view.

"Oh, I see, well I'd love to." Chloe nodded. "But I have to return to Paris. My dazzling job as a famous actress is waiting for me. Bye." The girl raced out of the door and Kana saw her strides slowed briefly, waiting for everyone to catch up. Gabriella and Kana joined the two officers, running immediately to the door.

"Oh my," Gabriella said. 'Chloe' cast an eye over her shoulder before returning to a full sprint.

"We have a suspect running on foot." The male officer shouted into his radio and barged passed everyone, running out to the police car parked outside.

"If she comes back for her things, please get in touch." The female officer hollered back looking over her shoulder as she ran. Both officers tumbled into the car. "She can't have gone far, Jim, she's on foot." The car door slammed and they drove away.

Gabriella closed the front door looking smug.

"Do you want to know something funny, Kana?"

"What?" "My daughter is both a genetic miracle, and a shape-shifting genius. Her DNA, when shifted, becomes entirely analogous to that which she is copying."

"Meaning?" Kana didn't understand.

"Meaning, her DNA won't show up on a single database."

"Is it safe to come out now?" Chloe peered from the stairs, grinning at Kana and Gabriella. "Just about thought I'd have to use vampire mind control."

Kana peered over in horror. "Wait. You have mind control? Then why did you kidnap me in the first place? "

"I'm just messing with you, darlin'. Don't all your vampire movie shows have mind control in them?"

Even Gabriella let out a tiny chuckle.

"Oh, for goodness' sake." Kana rolled her eyes but there was still a smile on her face.

10

The night rolled out across the sky like a new black velvet carpet. It glittered with stars the likes of which Kana had never seen before from the centre of town. Even so, her focus clung to the cool ground beneath her bare feet.

With the kitchen's plumbing and gas fixtures becoming the center of attention , the back door of the small bed and breakfast had yet to be replaced, The unsecured portal left Kana's exit into the garden unobstructed.

After her defiance toward her mother, no one seemed to care.

Kana was free.

She stood on the outside step wearing Chloe's bubblegum pink pyjamas, peering into the warm night air. A bitter sweet fragrance wafted over from the flowerbeds. Kana inhaled the floral scent; lilies. She'd always liked lilies, but in the darkness she could barely see their silhouettes.

Standing outdoors again without worry struck her as an alien sensation after so long being stuck inside. Her mended leg no longer impaired movement, and an unspoken truce was held between her, Gabriella, and her house-mates. Plus, for the first time in years, her mother's ten o' clock curfew carried no meaning.

She let the balmy air brush her long dark curls astray before stepping further into the garden. Her feet liked the cool moisture of soft grass. The light breeze helped to calm her. Curiosity about the garden and the rest of the house that was now technically her home tickled at the edges of her mind, and a little taste of freedom after being cooped up felt glorious.

"Gorgeous night, ain't it, lass?" Vincent's voice made her jump, and the resulting chuckle from him brought a scowl to her face. She couldn't see him out in the dark, but a pungent vegetal smell invaded her nostrils.

"Are you smoking?" She asked, squinting.

"Aye."

"Is that marijuana?"

"Aren't you fancy? I'm smoking weed, aye. If you don't like it, go inside."

"That's not what I meant." Kana snapped, a little harsher than she'd intended. "I meant what if Gabriella found out?" She still could not see the wolf man, which made her uncomfortable. Had he meant to sneak up on her, or has she inadvertently intruded on his alone time? She looked around, searching for the source of his voice.

"Gabriella knows." Vincent chuckled. "She pretends not to, of course, and as long as I don't draw the police to the door, or any attention, she's fine with just about anything. You, lass, have drawn more attention in a week than this ol' dog's brought in his entire time here."

She cringed; he had a point.

He moved slightly and Kana found him. His eyeshine, just like an animal's, reflected the light from an upstairs window. She walked toward him across the lawn, hesitantly. Her bare feet were tender, but the grass remained soft.

The red light from Vincent's joint winked in the night. His eyes glittered once more and she stopped. From closer up, the hazy silhouette of the wolf man appeared, leaning against the large five foot fence that ringed the border of the garden. He stood, head and shoulders above it.

"You ever smoked the green, lass?" His voice seemed to growl, but perhaps it was just the smoke in his lungs.

"Never. "

"So, away back inside then, like a good little girl who doesn't run away from home and smoke bad things with big bad wolves, and drink bad booze."

"I could, though. If I wanted to." Kana's hand found her hip, defiantly. "But I don't like it."

"How d'ye know you wouldn't like it if you never try it? Go on, then. Take a draw."

Kana paused. "Coward." Vincent teased. She could hear the grin in his voice.

"I am not. I just can't see. It's way too dark."

"Heh. Humans." Vincent chuckled. "I forget you lot are so blind in the dark. Hold on, lass." Vincent's form bustled passed her, his hand brushing one shoulder to stop himself from knocking her over as he did so. With a click, the outside porch light illuminated the well-kept garden in an amber glare. Though still in monochrome, the shape of the garden, the flowerbeds, and the shorn lawn could be seen in much finer detail.

"How's that, lass?"

"Better. I won't go banging into stray wolves in the night."

Vincent grinned and approached her. "Shame about that, eh? Here." He handed her the joint. "Give it a go. One little puff won't sully ye."

"Is that what you said to the three little pigs?"

Vincent barked out another low laugh and took her hand in his, tugging it up to her lips. "Take a deep breath, love. Inhale, and don't cough. Hold it for three seconds. Release it, and close your eyes."

Kana's stomach twirled at his words. She did as he asked, inhaled deep. The burn of the smoke scraped hot against her throat. It tickled too. Resisting the urge to cough was a battle. Nerves gripped her and she released her breath early. It caught in her throat as a coughing fit that nearly doubled her over. Vincent skillfully plucked the joint from her fingers before she could drop it. Her head tilted up, eyes watering.

"Very good, but not quite, now try again." His fingers pressed the lit joint to her lips once more. "Breathe in."

She took a deep draw, her eyes trapped in his. The red flared at the end of the joint.

"Hold."

Kana swallowed as a distraction, her lungs burned. Vincent shook his head.

"Breathe out. All of it."

Kana sighed out the air in her lungs. A rush of dizziness swept over her with her next breath. Her head rolled. Vincent's grin only grew larger. As she wobbled, he reached out to steady her.

"Now close your eyes, lass. Just relax."

Once more, she did as he told her. For a split second, she wondered if he was going to kiss her. Instead, he let go of her shoulders before her eyes slid open and staggered back.

"How's it feel to be free of your mother? Pretty good, ain't it?"

"Yeah." Kana wheezed. She coughed. At first it was a tiny cough, and then her sides racked with a series of almost choking noises as her lungs tried to clear themselves. She bent over double and Vincent's chuckle returned. He did, however, slap her gently on the back.

"Every time, lass. Happens on everyone's first try. You did pretty good though. Fancy another go?"

"No thanks. That's plenty." Kana shook her head and wiped her eyes from coughing so hard. She pinned her dizziness down to the cannabis, but Vincent's words did send a whoop of excitement through her. "Yeah, it does feel good to be free of my mum. Feels like an adventure. And for the first time in my life, I'm in charge."

"Well, I think you made the right choice, lass." The wolf man nodded, curling his arm around Kana's shoulder and tugging her closer to his chest. His arm and body against her almost suffocated her in heat. "Stay here with us. We'll keep you safe."

His face was inches from hers and littered with tiny scars only visible from her curled position in his arms. He must have caught her looking.

"Gabriella did that one," he mumbled, reaching up to run his thumb along the white line running up his cheek, "Sliced it open with a French rapier, back in the day."

Kana watched him and felt curious about who Vincent used to be.

"The day?" She focused on his mouth. "Oh, we go back some time, me and her. Used to pillage a few ships here and there back in the Caribbean in the eighteen hundreds. You think the fighting is bad now, lass, you should have seen us back then. She used to beat the shit out of me."

"You were sailors?"

"Nah." He beamed at her. "Pirates. You know: stolen rum, fenced cargo, the whole stinkin' menagerie of scum. Gabriella was a live wire, back before she had the kid. She had a passion for taking things too far."

Kana arched both brows, and tried to pull away. Her stomach knotted. She didn't understand why that caused her such concern.

"So are you two are. y'know?"

"Nah. Well, once but that ship's set sail. Why?" He leaned closer. Kana's heart beat hammered in her chest. "Is that something you'd like?"

Kana shook her head. "Nope," she wrinkled her nose in a devilish grin, "Gabriella's a bit too muscular for me." It took all her control not to giggle.

Vincent narrowed his brows. His eyes danced with mischief.

"What about me?"

"Oh, was that what you meant?" Kana felt bold. She pressed her hands against his chest. "Well, I always wanted a puppy. Maybe in time Gabriella can train you to be a half decent guard dog, hey?"

"Ruff." Vincent growled. Kana felt fire in her cheeks as his voice rumbled through her. Pulled so close against him there was little space between them. Her eyes flickered to the bristle on his upper lip. She wanted to bite that lip.

"Maybe I'll bark every time you're in danger. "

He had leaned closer. "Maybe I'll listen." She breathed the words out. Her face swelled with heat. She wanted to kiss him.

"Ruff." The wolf man's breath touched her lips and she swallowed hard wishing she'd agreed to another draw to steady her nerves. Her eyes closed.

"You two are positively revolting." Barney's drawl slithered out from the kitchen door and Kana's eyes popped open. Embarrassed, she leapt from the wolf man and hastily fixed her hair. The gaunt figure lingered in the doorway, folded arms and a disgusted sneer on his face. Even Vincent growled.

"What do you want Barney?"

"Nothing. Merely wondering how such an interspecies relationship would work. That said, if you and Gabriella can pro-create, I'm sure you can manage with this base creature."

Kana's head swivelled toward Vincent.

"Ah, are we still keeping that a secret from the little tag-along?" Barney looked proud of himself. "You see, some pets love their owners more than others, and this little 'puppy', as you called him, loved Gabriella enough to hump her leg a few times. Well," the ghoulish man bubbled rasping laughter, "not her leg. Definitely not her leg."

"Barney," Vincent growled. The noise set Kana's neck hair on end and she took a step back away from both men.

"And, against all odds, voila, the little shape-shifter was born. Of course, puppies aren't really good guard dogs are they, Vincent? Because he won't even acknowledge the child, let alone help raise her."

"We've been through this, Barney. That's not it. Gabby wanted the kid, not me. She didn't want Lola to know."

"So poor little Lola has had nought to consider a father. Good luck with getting high, Kana. I'm sure your mother will just love to hear about that." Barney shot them a caustic look and disappeared into the kitchen.

Kana could not meet Vincent's eyes. Nor could Vincent meet hers.

"I have to go inside." Kana stated. Vincent nodded and took another puff on his joint.

"Have a good night, Kana." He said stiffly.

The awkwardness of the scene in the garden left Kana with a bitter feeling in her throat. She had no doubt that Barney's intentions were to do exactly as he had succeeded in doing. Embarrassment ballooned in her stomach, along with shame, guilt, and the anxiety that everyone would know she almost kissed Vincent. She headed straight to her room and paused at her door.

Maybe Barney had lied about Vincent being Lola's father. After all, Barney's sole intention was to remove Kana from the house, one way or another. The only salvation Kana could see was that, as long as Gabriella remained in charge, he would not outright kill her.

Kana wondered just how old each of these creatures really was. Gabriella didn't appear to be any older than her mid thirties. Vincent only seemed to be in his twenties. But Chloe had been seventeen when she became a vampire. That the others had supernatural longevity too seemed completely plausible.

Another thought crossed Kana's mind, now that she had left the situation; a thought she didn't feel entirely comfortable with. Vincent had tried to say Gabriella didn't want Lola to know he was the father. That didn't make sense. Except perhaps for protecting her daughter from his taste for practically every recreational substance he could lay his hands on.

It didn't seem right to meddle, but Kana reasoned that Gabriella should know what Barney was saying. If Lola's father was meant to stay a secret, then Barney deserved to have his mouth shut by Gabriella.

She climbed up to the second floor and paused, uncertain which door was Gabriella's. The only reasonable thing was to knock on a few, and pray none belonged to Barney.

Most of the doors were unlocked. They lead into quaintly decorated bedrooms with double beds, at least one wardrobe and chest of drawers, a full length mirror and one or two windows depending on the layout. They all had en-suite bathrooms.

"Gabriella?" She called softly, her voice half a whisper.

A quick peer in a slightly open door revealed a room that had been claimed and she slipped inside for a better look.

A bouquet of scents: chocolate, rum, and a strange thick floral scent, hovered in the air like a miasma. Not merely sweet, the smell had earthy tones. She breathed deep, taking in the delicious smell. She reeled, her head spinning as she stumbled toward the bed and sat down to regain her bearings, wondering if the weed had began to redouble its effect. At least the room was vacant.

Well not precisely vacant, just unoccupied for the moment.

Whose room was it?

She debated leaving quickly. Having learned that the wolf man and the lady of the house had both been pirates together, the giant map of the world that engulfed three quarters of one wall meant this room belonged to either Vincent or Gabriella. It smelled lovely.

Perhaps this was the lady's room.

Something smooth took hold of the edges of her mind. She felt strange. The weed was stronger than she'd originally imagined. Her head seemed to be at the center of a nebula of warmth and softness, and the earthy, floral scent had grown sweeter in her nostrils.

She allowed herself to be distracted, giggling as the enjoyment of exploring this room hit her like that bubbly, earthy sweet scent. Her eyes landed on a tiny fabric chest, a black jewellery box, decorated in gold brocade on the bedside table. So Gabriella's room, then? Not Vincents. She giggled at the image of the lumbering wolf-man poised over a jewelry box, his big fingers plucking daintily at wee baubles.

She ran her hands along it, feeling every bump beneath her fingertips. It made her shiver. Up went the attached lid and she peered inside.

Trinkets. Gold. Just as she expected. So pretty. Each piece would surely be worth a small fortune, but the urge to steal never crossed her mind. Not much of anything could cross the muddy field her mind had become. No, she simply ran her fingers through the gold and silver chains as though they were sand, and closed the lid again. Placing it gently back on the bedside table, she suddenly felt exhausted.

Kana lay down. Her head plopped back against the pillow, luxuriating on the soft bed sheets. Yes, they were silken soft and cool on her skin, more Egyptian cotton, and the air spilled out of her in a long, relaxed sigh.

She could smell the wolf on them. So that answered that.

Kana was beyond caring. The stomach turning reek of old beer, the predominant scent of male sweat, removed all doubt of which body lay on these sheets by nights.

He is still intolerable, she decided, although for the life of her, she could no longer remember why. Her limbs sprawled and she sighed again. She ran her fingers through her hair, letting the long curls slide through her hands. That felt nice too. Bare feet, slightly damp from the grass now slid along the gloriously pliant, cool sheets. Her head was spinning.

Deep breaths.

She closed her eyes and out trickled another amused giggle.

One of the pillows lay large and plump at her side; she pulled it toward her, hugging its refreshing satin into her body. The door creaked further open. Kana didn't notice. The pillow felt sensuous against her curves. *What the hell am I doing?*

A part of her brain observed that her behavior had gone to the ridiculous; but at the same time it felt good, it felt right. Her hands stroked down the pillow till they met level with her hips and she pulled the pillow in tight. Her right hand left the pillow to stroke one of her hips.

What if this was Vincent instead of the pillow?

An amusing thought, one that burst the second she heard his voice in the doorway. "Side-tracked by the incense, eh?" He chuckled.

The door clicked behind him. Kana's eyes, heavy and warm, reluctantly slid open. It seemed funny to have him here, when she had just been wanting him. She giggled, still hugging her pillow of choice that bore his scent and seemed to hug her back. She watched as he headed towards a large incense burner in the other end of the room that she hadn't noticed, and blew it out. "That's what I get for trying to prepare my room for hot-boxing. You okay, lass?"

Kana gave a very fluid nod, before resting her head on the pillow. Hot-boxing? Did that mean more drugs?

"Is thath erm smell?" She managed, her head feeling fuzzy. Again, one hand reached to her face, pushing dark curls away from her cheeks. They tickled. "Spell can't smell the spell," she giggled.

"Aye." He nodded, stepping towards her. "Try and clear your head. What you doing in my room, Kana?"

Kana didn't have a clue what he was talking about. Her head was too fuzzy, but as he took a few steps towards the bed, Kana sat up, leaned forward and reached for his hand, trying to tug him closer. His heated skin felt good on hers. Calming, relaxing, and oh so soothing. She could feel her body heating up at his touch. The feeling of arousal nipping between her thighs.

"You should lie down with me," She said, smiling. Her head lolled back, her body tugged back toward the satin sheets like a force of gravity.

Vincent grinned but stood his ground.

"You're out your head, lass. How long you been in here?"

"Long 'nough t'spell the smell? Heh." Her head lolled on the pillows again. "Long enough to d'scover I don't want to move. I like i'n 'ere. Iss fluffy. Like Christmas."

"Christmas," He chuckled. "Come on, you dozy cow." He leant forward, tugging her up and lifted her utterly relaxed body into his arms. She clung, but only just barely, arms flopping over his shoulders and fingers lacing together around his neck.

"Vincent." That she enunciated clearly. "Do you know, I am completely new to this, so you be a gentleman."

"Is that right?" Vincent replied in exaggerated mock surprise. He carried her out of his room, one hand fastening her to his chest, the other clicking the door closed.

"Yessir, Mister Puppy-Man." The word slurred out. "I am a bespectacled, um the testicles; no. No no no. I am a respectable young woman, and I," the rest of that thought faded and required too much effort. She curled up, her face resting on Vincent's broad shoulder. His skin smelled just like his sheets. He hoisted her higher, carrying her downstairs to her room.

"God and all his saints 'n' angels add preservatives to us. Gabriella sees you like this, she'll skin me alive and turn me into a rug."

"Nah- Oof." Kana grunted as Vincent threw her onto her own bed. She bounced once, flat on the bed.

"There. You'll be fine. Little woozy, but shit happens. Feel groggy at all? Sick?"

Kana tried to shake her head but that was too much like hard work, so instead she repeated herself.

"Nah." She wiped her mouth of drool.

"Alright then," He cautiously backed up to leave. "Stay out of my room."

"Wait."

"What?"

"I'm thirsty."

"Well, there's a bathroom in here." Vincent nodded to the other door.

"Please?"

Vincent sighed, rolled his eyes and paced across the room to fetch a glass of water. He returned with a tumbler fill of cold water, passing it to her. She gulped it down with vigour.

"Is that all, your majesty?" He teased. "Or would she like a foot rub and all?"

"Nah, I'z good. You, bad. V'ry bad." Another giggle hit. "But I likes it."

The left side of Vincent's lip hooked up. His thin blonde whiskers bristled. He puffed out his amusement and turned to leave.

"Wait."

"Aye?"

"Come lie down 'round me. "

"Lass, you're baked. Sort your knickers and yourself. I ain't pillaging your knickers while you're doped up. Do you hear me in there?"

Kana whined, persistent. "No, I had a question." Vincent waited. She couldn't, for the life of her, remember what she had wanted to ask. She burst into a cackle of laughter, eyes lazy as she grinned at him.

Vincent sighed and dropped down onto the bed.

"You happy now, lass?"

"Yeah." Kana nodded, putting her hand on his bare wrist. "You got big arms."

"Aye. From hoisting sails, lifting daft drug soaked wenches, and carting all the treasure I can git my hands on."

"Whuzzamahmmph," Kana rubbed her forehead when Vincent laughed and she tried again: "What. Was. That. Incense?" The light dosage of the drug was beginning to wear off.

"My own little blend bit of opium, ayahuasca and a few other bits and bobs." He shrugged. "When you got a lot of time, you get bored with the plain stuff."

"I didn't even know you could get such things outside the eighteenth century; opium I mean." her words were flowing easier. Easier, but not easily; her thoughts still moved slow. She didn't have a clue what the other thing he'd said meant.

"I know a guy."

"Right," Kana did not ask what kind of "guy" that might be.

They lay there for a while, letting her head clear. His arm had draped around her and Kana snuggled up against his side, boldly laying her knee over his outstretched leg. She finally sighed and felt more like herself again, just pleasantly happy.

He must have known. Of course he did. He could sense it.

"So do you wanna give me a hint, lass? What sordid reason did you have for waltzing into my room?"

Kana gave a shrug. "The door was open, I was looking for Gabriella. It was fifty-fifty it was her room or yours."

"You won't be finding her in my room, unless she suddenly developed a craving for opium, same as you did."

Kana shook her head. It was still thick with haze, the pleasant echo of the drug washing through her in dreamy hot pulses. "I didn't. Not really. It was sort of an accident." She sat up now, finding her sense of balance and trying to maintain it. "Am I going to overdose?"

"You're alright. Just make sure its out your system before ye come to breakfast." He rose from the bed, deciding it was time to leave. "So what you think? Was it as good as you always hoped 'n' feared it would be?"

"What?"

"The quality, was it pure?"

"I wouldn't know. First time, same as the marijuana."

Vincent rolled his eyes and pursed his lips. For a moment he said nothing, but his expression was both guilty and frustrated. "Aye. Talk about a crash course then." He reasoned. "Right, so, ehm, let's not tell Gabby about this, hmm? Our little secret."

Kana knew she should have been furious, worried even, that Vincent was hoarding such things and even smoking drugs without Gabriella's permission. After all. It was her bed and breakfast. But for now, she only found Vincent's anxiety rather entertaining. He looked as though his mind lay trapped between contrition and worry. Although, a part of her found it odd he forgot to stop it burning when he'd left the room. She ran her hands through her hair, reality hitting her once more.

"What did Barney mean outside about Lola?" She mumbled pressing her palm to her dysfunctional forehead. "Was gonna ask Gabriella, but I didn't find her."

Vincent frowned, his eyebrows drawing down into a solid firm line.

"He's right. Lola's my daughter. But Gabriella doesn't want her to know that. It's just as simple as that."

"Why?"

"Drop it, Kana. It's not a thing I wish to discuss." "Please tell me. I can keep a secret." She couldn't drop it. "Please? I won't mention the dog jokes again."

Vincent softened by a fraction. "I like the dog jokes, lass. Least, I do from you."

"Tell me? Please?"

Vincent sighed and lay back across the bed again, although this time Kana curled up her legs to give him space.

"You see, lass, it's like this. Me and Gabriella lost contact for many years. We met up again, I needed a place to stay. She was all melancholy for the old days; there ain't no pirates around here. We ended up together and by sheer luck, misfortune, or whatever you want to call it, Lola happened."

"But ?"

"We're friends. Weren't nothing but a solution to loneliness, some excitement to cure her boredom. Gabby's no soft-hearted no fool and ain't looking for love, least not from a wild wolf hound like me." Vincent gnawed his lip, remembering and shook his head, scowling.

"Did it last long?"

He released a barking scoff, "Not even a whole night. The Ice Queen gave me the boot, said I made her bed stink like a sweaty dog."

"That's cold." Especially since Kana liked the smell of wolf on his satiny sheets. That memory was seared into her mind. No opium would remove it.

He gave a shrug, "We moved on. That was that. Never thought more of it. Didn't even know she was pregnant. She told me I could stay, but to keep my yap shut. So, that was that, too. Never even knew that wee babe was coming 'til Gabby couldn't hide the bump no more. Tis her business, she says, hers alone. I agreed. But I stayed. 'Tis right, regardless of Gabriella's ice."

"Oh." Kana's face fell, suddenly feeling a lot more sober. "I'm so sorry."

"Don't tell me you're sorry Kana. I don't want to hear it." The wolf man pulled a lighter from his pocket and flicked the trigger, letting the tiny flame wobble back and forth. "I don't need to hear it, anyway. We don't feel badly about how it's worked out, not between us anyhow. But every now and again Barney brings it up, the bastard. He thinks he's rubbing salt in a wound. He's not, but he enjoys getting on my nerves. If knowing about Lola makes you uncomfortable, then get over it. I did."

Kana didn't know what to say. She felt awful for him, but he didn't want to hear her sympathy. She said nothing as he stood and stalked out of the room.

"Once more, good night, Kana. Sleep well, lass."

"Good night. Thanks for talking to me, Vincent."

He shrugged, "Just keep yer yap shut, eh?"

"Sure."

It was only as she curled up to sleep, that Kana had another thought, and it broke her heart to think about it.

Did Vincent abuse his healing this much with drugs and alcohol before Gabriella had Lola? She suspected the answer was no. A wolf's heart was a deep and dangerous place.

11

"How long do we have to tolerate them prowling outside our house?" Barney growled, standing by the living room window. He watched the police car outside. It sat in complete silence, the officers occasionally walking the length of the street to stretch their legs.

"I'm not certain. Until they decide Lola is outside their jurisdiction, I would suppose." Gabriella sipped her tea. "I wonder how far she has gone? Regardless, Chloe will have to stay indoors and try not to draw attention to herself." She peered outside, hooking the curtains back for a better look.

Kana glanced up from her curled position on the couch, watching television, and listened with worry of her own. Despite the fact Chloe's blood theft was of her own volition, Kana felt partially responsible for getting the vampire noticed.

Yet, this awkward scrutiny by the police still felt better than being tucked away in her mother's house. "Maybe when they realise she's in France, they'll leave and not come back." Kana offered.

"Stubborn bastards," Vincent growled from the hall. "Wish I could just tear right into the lot of them."

"Of course." Barney held his arms out wide. "Because that would make things so very much better. Why tolerate two of them when we could face down two regiments of them?"

Vincent narrowed his brows. "There's a reason I said 'wish' not 'will'."

"We had best hope they pick up and leave before Vincent's wish becomes a reality." Gabriella pulled back from the window. Barney gave a 'hmm' in response.

"A reality?" Kana turned to Vincent. "Why?"

"It's the wolf in me, lass." Vincent said with a shrug. "Full moon rolls around, well, I get a bit unpredictable. Turn back into a beastie, come gods or government."

Kana's smirk bloomed into a huge grin. "It's your time of the month."

Gabriella tried to hide her mirth behind an itch of her nose. Barney sounded as if he might choke on something.

"Don't." Vincent growled. His moustache bristled. "It's not funny, lass."

"I'm sorry." Kana could not resist. "Are you having it now?"

"Kana, blessed me. Stop." Vincent grimaced. Barney rolled his eyes.

"It does last a full week, cábron." Gabriella glanced at the pair over her shoulder. "Maybe the girl has a point."

"Ah'm not listening to this." Vincent growled. "I do not menst— do that."

Kana giggled now. Making him squirm was fun. "Do what, Vincent?"

"That thing lassies do."

"Which is?" She pressed, enjoying the sour look he threw her.

"Bleed." Barney offered, dryly, trying to silence her.

"I'm not saying it." Vincent whined, stalking off into the kitchen. After inadvertently getting her high last night, he deserved a little ribbing. Kana jumped to her feet and hurried after him, his sulking was far too perfect not to antagonise. She followed him outside, musing on the ashen state of the kitchen as she passed through. It was probably a good thing the police hadn't checked there.

"You're not scared of a little blood, are you Vincent?"

"I'll show you your own blood in a minute if it'll shut you up," the wolf man said dryly, but by now she knew he was all bark, no bite; at least toward her. Kana bit back a giggle. Vincent gave her a bemused look.

"Say it, go on, I dare you."

"You trying to get me with that peer pressure, lass? Go on, sod off." Vincent pulled a lighter and a cigarette from his pocket. It was a brand new one this time and he flicked the lighter several times trying to light it.

"So you're allowed to use peer pressure and I'm not?"

"Aye."

"Well, that's not very fair." Kana jutted out her hip and curled her hand upon it. Vincent's eyes darted down and then back up, appreciating her figure in the jeans and smooth-fitting red tee-shirt she had borrowed from Chloe today. Determined to stay sour, he puffed out a breath of smoke.

"Life's not fair, lass. You'll get used to it."

True. Life wasn't fair. "Smoking's bad for you." Kana stated.

"Yup, just like everything else. Y'know, there's one thing in life that has a one hundred percent mortality rate."

"And what's that?"

"Life."

Kana didn't bother to argue.

Gabriella's head poked out of the gaping hole in the kitchen wall where the back door should be. "Kana," her voice was dark with warning. "You're not bothering my guest, are you?"

Clearly Vincent didn't need her protection. He scowled at the intrusion. "Guest? You mean talking bank account, with the amount you charge me in rent." He muttered around the cigarette in his mouth. It wobbled dangerously. "Leave her, she's fine."

Gabriella glanced at each of them, giving her head a small shake.

"Well, make sure she doesn't inhale any of that."

"Gabby, it's a bloody cigarette, not fucking heroin."

"Yes, but she's human." Gabriella's arms folded over her chest.

Kana swore she saw a challenge in the ice queen's eyes.

"Gabby, what do you take me for? I'm hardly gonna give the lass something I'm not meant to."

"I wouldn't take it if he did." Kana added, with all the sincerity she could muster.

Gabriella's eyes narrowed and she watched the two of them. Kana feared she could see right through their words. Maybe she knew what had happened in Vincent's room, or at least big-mouth Barney had blabbed about what catching them out in the yard, before that.

"Fine. The pair of you behave, then."

"Always," Vincent mumbled.

Gabriella disappeared back inside. When Kana decided the coast was clear, she burst into giggles again. Even Vincent grinned down at her.

"You know, for a second, I swear she knew." Kana said.

"No doubt she does." Vincent took another draw and released it slowly. "There's little our Gabriella doesn't know about her house, but she doesn't pry. I'll have to thank her for that sometime."

"So if you two have known each other for so long, you two must be pretty, um, advanced in years."

Vincent snorted out another chuckle. "That a fancy way to say we're old as hell?"

Kana shrugged. "If you like."

"Lemme see, now I would have been born, in a manner o' speakin', in the year of yer lord One Thousand, Seven Hundred 'n' Two. Do your math." Vincent nudged her with his elbow, grinned at her shock and flicked his ash.

Kana's eyes widened. "Being a werewolf makes you immortal?"

"Aye, and you'd think 'twas a gift. It's just annoying. Getting ID for anything is a bugger. Gabriella drives, but only 'cause she got her hotel up. Birth certificates are damn near impossible, and you got all those forms. Eh, it's complicated. After a hundred years or so, you have to start over. Do it a few times and you just get tired of doin' it. I haven't officially existed for a good long time now."

It sounded almost impossible. "So, I bet you don't even have a passport."

"Never did have one. I stopped bothering about paperwork before that manner of paperwork existed." Vincent leaned back against the side of the house and cricked his neck from side to side. "Sure you want to live here, lass? Not to speak ill of my host, this is better than home for me. But livin' out there in the wide world again, that's what I fancy. Offer me a ship on the waves and wind in the sails, I'd run to it in a heartbeat."

"What about, " Kana hesitated, unsure whether or not to pry. Though the memory of what Vincent had told her felt vague and foggy in hindsight, there was no denying his negative reaction.

"In a heartbeat, Kana." He repeated. Kana pursed her lips.

"Fair enough," but she said to her shoes. If a ship on the high seas, all alone and far away brought him more comfort than being here, she realized what a deep disappointment his life had become. It tore at her heart. But he was loyal. Despite it all, he had stayed. Vincent watched her for a second, then crushed the burnt out cigarette butt against the wall and let it drop.

"Rest easy, lass." He grinned and patted her shoulder, moving closer as they talked. "It's not your worry. Right?"

But she did worry. Somewhere between that giant wolf pouncing on her in the front yard and last night's heart to heart, Vincent had become very important to Kana.

"Besides," he did that nonchalant shrug her perfected, "The wee thing is nearly grown. Don't need coddlin' n'fussin' no more. 'Tis fierce and smart, just like her Mum."

On that, she did agree.

"Kana." Gabriella's voice suddenly rang loud from the hallway, and the pair sprang apart guiltily. Vincent and Kana shot each other a look and the wolf man pressed his finger to his lips. Kana grinned. Gabriella's face appeared in the blackened doorway once more.

"There's a visitor at the door for you."

That confused Kana. As she puzzled out who would be visiting her at Gabriella's, she hoped dearly that her mother hadn't returned. She followed the Spanish woman into the hall. Her sister stood there playing with the bell at the reception desk under the stairs.

"Kana." She beamed and ran to hug her. Despite Karen's enthusiasm, Kana flinched and patted her shoulder warily. She had missed her sister, but at the same time, stll clearly recalled their last interaction. "I missed you. Mum said you wouldn't come home and I thought you'd been kidnapped or something awful."

Kana heard a shuffle from upstairs.

She ignored it for now and focused on Karen. "No, I've moved out." Kana announced. *And borrowing a vampire's clothes till I get my own back.*

That perky attitude abruptly shifted, proving the friendliness totally fake. "Really? That's what you think you've done?"

"It seems self-evident to me. I'm here, not there." Kana folded her arms in defiance. " I'm progressing. I'm out of Mum's hair. I'm doing well here. I'm happy."

"We both know that's a lie, Kana. All you're doing is embarrassing Mum. The neighbours are asking where you are. Mum's mortified. I hope you're pleased. They're gonna think she's an unfit mother or your shacking up with some random guy."

"They thought otherwise when I was still living with my mother?" She let out a scoff. "Tell them where to go."

"You won't get anywhere in life telling people to disappear if you don't like what they're saying Kana. I know you don't want to hear it, you never want to hear anyone tell you that you're wrong."

"I might be more receptive if you two occasionally said anything except that."

"But people's opinions matter. You need to start taking care of yourself. Not expecting others to do it for you."

Now Kana was furious. "Which is exactly why I'm here. Not there. That's what I'm doing now; taking care of myself. No-one asked you to come ind me. If you don't like this, just leave," Kana felt her blood boil. Her sister always did know the right words to push buttons. "Just leave, right now, Karen."

"I can't. Mum expects me to do the right thing and bring you home."

The little margin of courtesy Kana fought to keep had trickled away. She took a deep breath. "Maybe, for once in her entire life, the world doesn't need to revolve around Mum. Maybe I'm doing this for my benefit, not just to spite her." "No." Karen wagged her finger and Kana fought the urge to break it. "No. You don't speak about her like that. That's really immature, Kana, running off like that. You're the oldest, you're supposed to be responsible. You need to get a job and stop sponging. Mum told me how you bad mouthed off to her in front of all these people. And what's worse, you want to stay here while the police are at the door, that's even more stupid."

Kana felt a strong arm push her to one side.

"Who the hell are you?" Vincent growled.

Karen stopped, and tilted her head, looking him up and down.

"Stop staring and start talking, lass."

He looked fierce and rather frightening, his shaggy blonde hair and piercing blue eyes adding to that effect, along with the fact his broad shoulders filled the doorway.

Kana felt a slight pang of jealousy at Vincent calling her sister "lass". That was her name, right? The wall mounted light looked like a great thing to hit Karen with.

"I'm Kana's sister. Now back to your room and leave us be. I have a rape whistle and I will use it."

"Use it, then." Vincent growled. "But if you do, I hope it tastes good because I'll make you eat it." The pair locked eyes, staring each other down. That feral look in Vincent's eyes had returned. Kana wasn't entirely sure if he wanted to eat her sister or paint the walls with her.

Good. She'd love to watch.

"You got a problem with me?" Karen asked stiffly, the other hand going to her hip. "When you don't even know me?"

"I know enough. By the look of it, you're as loose with those hips as you are with that tongue of yours and you're about as welcome as a boil on my arse." Vincent sneered. "And I can smell your fear. You stink of it."

Karen pulled a disgusted look and tsked. Kana noticed just how much like their mum she looked right now. "Karen." She took care to enunciate every last syllable clearly. "It's time for you to leave."

"Don't be silly, Kana. I just got here. I have a point to make."

"You already made it. Just leave." Kana insisted. "Now."

Frustration at Mummy's Little Princess who was once again belittling her had reached its pinnacle. Even blood related, Karen could only be tolerated so far. The urge to beat the arrogance out of her grew and pulsed in Kana's blood. Her fists clenched tight.

Shadowing over her, Vincent made a noise and she knew he sensed it.

If Kana shouted 'kill' would he do it?

Probably.

But Karen was oblivious of the danger. "Do you have any idea how rude you are? Besides, this is not your house, Kana. You can't say things like that to people when you don't own the property. It's infantile. I can't believe how much growing up you still have to do."

"We can't all be Little Miss Perfect." Kana snapped. "Get out."

" I'm not going home without you. Stop screaming for attention and just come home. Stunts like this are the reason Dad left."

Kana could contain herself no longer. Her head spun with pure rage. Kana had been six when her mother moved away with the two of them; Karen, four. Neither of the girls remembered their father well, but the rule remained not to talk about it.

Karen had broken that rule.

Kana launched herself at Karen, sending their bodies sprawling to the ground with a thump. Karen's head narrowly missed the laminate and in seconds the natural sibling scrapping reached its peak. The pair screamed and hissed as fingers found hair, nails scratched faces, and legs kicked out. The two slammed together. Karen's manicured nails tore down Kana's cheek, sending burning pain through her face.

 Kana reached out and ripped out a clump from Karen's neat, tight ponytail, rat tailing the ends and Karen immediately did the same. Both pulled hard at hair, hissing and throwing insults. Kana bit her sister's arm as it passed her face. They rolled around the hallway floor. Karen screamed and threw her elbow into Kana's ribs.

"Christ." Vincent reached out to grab one of them. "Kana Karen" He finally landed a hand on Kana and hauled her back, but she was still screaming profanities at the top of her lungs.

"Let me go. I'm going to fucking kill the bitch." Kana screamed.

"*Que Mierda*? What is going on, Kana?" The Spanish woman snapped, hauling her sister back.

"That little wench was just leaving." Vincent insisted, pulling Kana's arms behind her back to stop her struggling.

"She was." Kana shouted. "And she's telling mum I'm never coming back. Ever."

"Kana, you're a selfish little brat and one day you're going to get your comeuppance. I hope you burn in hell." Karen yelled, the vehemence of her anger almost jolting her right out of Gabriella's arms.

"Go fuck yourself." Kana spat back.

"Always so eloquent."

"Ladies," Gabriella roared. Her fingertips turned to ice for a moment. Karen didn't see it, but she surely felt that icy grip on her shoulders. Her voice demanded silence. "Karen, please leave. Your visit is over. And it's your last." She escorted Karen to the door.

"Whatever." Kana's little sister slipped free of Gabriella's grip. She yanked open the front door and turned heel, pausing long enough to hiss, "Just think about someone else for a change, Kana. Your actions have consequences."

She banged the door shut with force.

"*Dios mio* my door." Gabriella sighed softly.

Vincent finally let Kana go.

"Easy, lass. Breathe, eh?"

Kana grit her teeth. Her cheek smarted from Karen's nails ripping the skin. She wanted to scream in frustration to force back any potential tears.

"I'm not selfish. I feel safe here, even if Barney hates me. It's better that life with them," she spat the last word, letting off steam.

She was so near tears, no one spoke.

She had dared to think leaving might help her mother and sister to lighten up; believed that space would make things easier. Karen's words had stabbed deep.

Gabriella pinched the bridge of her nose with her thumb and first finger.

"I like to think," she said, her eyes closing. "That I am a patient woman but I cannot, will not, tolerate that intrusion in my house. No. Not for one minute."

"I'm sorry."

"Not you, Kana." Gabriella took in another deep breath. "There was really no need for an invasion like that. What on earth was she trying to achieve?"

Kana couldn't answer. She was stuck between tears and rage.

"I think, " A tiny voice trilled from upstairs. Kana looked up to find an uneasy Yula and a horrified Chloe peering down. Of course everyone would be watching.

"Kana," she finished for Yula, "how do I put this politely? Your sister is a heap of crap." Chloe sighed.

"Yes, yes," Yula nodded, her red hair flaming around her face. "Maybe she should have been eaten at birth."

Kana gave a weak smile, "I have to agree." But Karen's hateful 's words clung in her head. If she stayed at home, her family thought her a burden, hated everything she did. At Gabriella's she was an outcast and an embarrassment. She couldn't win either way.

Barney, who had been lurking in the living room, rolled his eyes.

"Always the centre of attention, aren't you, Kana?" He sneered from the living room doorway, gazing at her with pure distaste.

Vincent grabbed Kana, to prevent her saying anything. "He's not worth it, lass. Zip yer' yap. Come on." Vincent growled. His hand was firm around Kana's waist as he hauled her close. "You say one more word, Barney, and I swear rules or no rules, I'll put you in a bucket of shite, head first."

"Si." Gabriella nodded. "And I'll let him."

Barney merely shrugged.

"Oh, dear" Yula looked worried, crouching lower behind the stair railing. Barney stormed up past her and Chloe. She ran after him. "Barney. Wait. "

"I hope she sets him on fire." Vincent said, tugging Kana tight against him, both arms wrapped around her back. His chest felt warm and safe, and she hid her face against it. Her shoulders shook with sorrow despite how hard she tried not to let the tears flow. Even here, her family could still wear her down.

Vincent was right. Life was not fair.

The nicest person in her life was a snarky werewolf.

How screwed up was that?

"Vincent. Don't antagonise him." Gabriella sighed. "I don't like this any more than you do."

"Then kick. Him. Out." Vincent's entire body rumbled with every enunciated word. "There's no reason he has to hover over you like he does. He could just as easily be skulkin' around a bog somewhere." Holding her protectively, Kana felt his hand slide through the tangles of her hair and cradle her head. The small, tender action set off more tears.

"Maybe I should go back." Kana mumbled. Her voice distorted against Vincent's chest, making it sound forlorn and small.

"Don't be daft. You're not going anywhere you don't want to."

"I agree. This is my house and I'll have no-one threaten my guests. Your mother and sister have no place here if they won't behave themselves." Gabriella folded her arms and frowned. "My guests have *some* leeway. Visitors have none."

Their gentility only brought more pain to Kana's tender heart.

"Ach," the wolf man grumbled, "you belong here, lass."

"Do I?"

"Sure. You were raised by vile vicious beasts," he chuckled, stroking her long brown curls again, "seems to me you fit right in."

She could have shouted, or stormed out and taken her anger out elsewhere but she didn't have to. Vincent would hold her till the anger dried up.

The room became awkwardly silent. Kana knew Chloe and Gabriella were still watching Vincent clutch her body to his chest, comforting while she cried. Suddenly, she didn't care what anyone thought. Werewolf or not, he had a heart. In her mind, that made him a better person than anyone she had known before coming here.

"You must all forgive me; I have to step out briefly. Chloe might be hungry." Gabriella stated.

"I could use a bite."

"Si, I will be back later." Gabriella beckoned Chloe into the kitchen. The vampire ran after her.

"What's she mean?" Kana sniffed, pulling away from Vincent to wipe her nose with the back of her hand. Her face was probably pink and her eyes were probably puffy, but she didn't care about that, either.

Vincent understood rejection and how deep it hurt. "Since Chloe's sick of animal blood, housebound, and pinching from the hospital is out, we're trying out a new thing called *Gabriella's blood*. She's a tough one, that Gabriella. That healing of hers."

"Yeah, wish I had that." Kana peered up. Vincent grinned and it made Kana suspicious. "What?"

"Come upstairs."

Kana hesitated.

He clearly sensed her apprehension, "Don't get the wrong idea, lass. I like ye' plenty, but now is not the time for that. I think you've earned another dose of my stuff. To help you relax and forget the awful ache inside for a little while."

"Yes. Okay." Kana nodded, definitely in the right frame of mind to do something stupid to her body. Vincent's drug concoction felt like the perfect antidote to her family and Barney.

She followed him upstairs, taking his hand as she did.

12

It was hours before Kana stirred. Darkness still blanketed the house. She blinked trying to find the source of the heat on her side. Her vision settled to reveal Vincent curled around her.

She didn't want to move.

She had little choice; the pressure on her bladder demanded relief. Still wearing yesterday's clothes, Kana peeled away from the sleeping heat source. Groggily, she headed to the bathroom to relieve herself.

When she returned, the wolf man blinked, but did not move from lying on his side, except for wiggling the fingers on one hand. "Ah, there you are. Come back. You're quite snuggly, lass." He opened his arms to show the empty space where she had slept. "I could sleep like this for days."

To prove it, he yawned huge.

"It's that heavy dose of *relief* you lit up last night before we

127

passed out, laughing like fools. I think you double-dosed. You're funny when you're high."

He gave her a wolfish grin, "Tis the company, lassie."

Kana liked that he relaxed enough with her to have fun. From Vincent, it was a supreme compliment. But something felt off today. Awkward; not anything between them, but something else was happening somewhere in the house. It was an odd instinct, but Kana felt the change in the air. "I think we have company downstairs."

Vincent's brow arched, clearly surprised she recognized something he already sensed. "Aye, we do. Stay up here with me. Tis trouble ye don't need. Or want." His fingers wiggled again, begging her to return. "Trust me. Come, Kana. Your place is here tonight. It's safe here."

She was dying to know. "Who is it?"

"Curious little bugger, ain't ye? Got a nose for trouble." He groaned, rolling onto his back to throw one burly arm across his blue eyes, "Fine, go satisfy your burning curiosity. Just remember, I warned ye."

"You aren't coming downstairs?"

"Hell, no." Within seconds he was breathing slow and deep again, fallen fast asleep.

After Vincent's warning, now she really did have a burning curiosity to know who was downstairs that the wolf man would so blatantly avoid. She stepped into the hall.

Voices filtered up to her from downstairs.

Vincent's door clicked as she closed it and a quiet murmur of voices echoed up from the living room. She followed the sound. At the bottom of the stairway she craned her neck around the door frame.

Sitting poker faced and poker straight in one chair, Gabriella watched the others around her. To her right, Yula wrung her hands nervously and Barney stood behind, hovering over the chair the red-head occupied.

The back of a head that Kana did not recognise sat in another seat. She couldn't see his face. Male, with a fuzz of semi-curled silver hair, he held a cup something warm. She inhaled lightly, testing the scent of the room. It was tea, very strong tea.

Yula peered up, looking pleasantly surprised. "Kana," she squealed, ceasing the wringing of her hands long enough to clap them together in excitement. Her appearance seemed to bring extreme enjoyment to the salamander. Whatever was happening before she came downstairs had gone on the back burner. Yula seemed to lose a decade from her expression. "We have a new guest."

Barney, naturally, did nothing more than raise an eyebrow and the corner of his mouth into a derisive sneer, clearly offended by her continued existence. Kana ignored him, but she felt his gaze land on her like lead.

The man put down his cup of tea and leaned back in his chair. "Are you going to enter room or not, child? Come, let me see human that has entire Montigo household so up in arms." He spoke without turning his head, his hands steepled in front of his chest. Kana's eyes flicked to Gabriella, whose head tilted in the briefest of nods. The ice queen had an anxious look on her face.

So Kana entered, slowly.

Vincent had said to stay upstairs. *It's safe here.* Maybe she should have listened. After all, he cared enough to protect her. But it was too late now. It occurred to her this man could be just as dangerous as Gabriella, Barney, or any other creature in this household.

She gave him a wide berth, taking a position closer to Gabriella, the lesser of the many evils in the room. Kana felt keyed up, sensing the tension in the room. It was impossible to tell whether her anxiety was due to her own apprehension over meeting another one of this motley crew within Gabriella's household, or if it was caused by Gabriella, Yula, and Barney's currently unsettled demeanour.

Kana's eyes met a dazzling green gaze.

The man's hairline tapered down into a curly silver beard that fairly engulfed his rosy face with a large Grecian nose, almond eyes and a generous mouth. Even for his age his was incredibly handsome, alarmingly so. In body and face he was a male perfection. Kana's cheeks flushed. As if sensing this, that mouth twitched at one corner, tugging up into a disarming smile that dried Kana's mouth in the space of a heartbeat.

"Kana Ingrid Lindqvist. I am right, yes?" The stranger spoke

with a purr of an accent only vaguely reminiscent of Gabriella's. En-
tranced, Kana momentarily lost her ability to speak, nodding. Her
face was on fire, and she could not look him in the eye. So she let
her gaze do the elevator ride from bottom to top, to bottom again.

He wore trainers; plain white canvas shoes, a thin t-shirt, and
plain crème cargo pants that stopped below his knee. Many pockets
decorated the trousers. There was no ignoring what they covered
either; another reason for Kana's face to fill with blood, and it wasn't
the only place. He was old enough to be her grandfather, yet he was
utterly alluring.

She was keenly aware of the charisma and power within the man.

"I am told you have met entire household due to," he gestured
with his hands, somewhat helpless for words, "situations regarding
our Chloe's drinking habits? Yes? Is a shame, real shame, they are
usually so well behaved." He shot a look at Barney. who did not meet
his eyes.

Kana looked at Gabriella for help. The immortal nodded help-
fully.

Why was everyone being so quiet? Sure, he was fun to look at,
and had a disarming, even grandfatherly way about him, but what
about introductions?

"Lola is not here at moment, I think."

"Yes, she is out." Gabriella answered, " My daughter is dealing
with the situation. Reasonably, I can assure you."

"Is good." The stranger gave a brief nod and sipped at his tea. "I
would have liked say hello to funny little one, but meh. She is working. So young to be working."

"Sorry, but," Kana interrupted, "who are you?"

The attractive stranger sent her another disarming smile. "I have
whole army of names. But maybe I give you easiest one. You may call
me Atlas. Please, sit."

Kana obeyed, shuffling toward the couch and settled down onto
it. With every passing moment she wished she had stayed upstairs.
Gabriella wrapped an arm around her shoulder. Fingers bit into her
shoulders, clearly as a warning.

"You wonder, maybe, what I can do. Probably you see everyone
here has powers you think are only from fairy tales?"

Kana decided he would be much cuter if he talked less. He seemed to enjoy the sound of his own voice far too much. When he bent forward to reach for his beverage once again, Kana's mouth opened, and while it wasn't quite the entire English language that tumbled from her lips, it wasn't too far short of it.

"Actually," Kana leaned toward the man, if he was a man at all. "Mostly I'm just wondering why the hell you sound Russian. Are you Russian?"

Atlas blinked, then barked laughter. "No, Kana. Not Russian. But is closest your mind can get, maybe. But you understand me, yes?"

"Right," Kana scowled. "As if this place wasn't bizarre already, now we've got Boris Badenov."

"Kana." Gabriella urged, voice half a growl. "Don't. Not with this one, *mierda*."

Barney blew air through pursed lips. Yula's gaze flicked to the floor. Awkwardly.

To everyone's surprise, Atlas gave a tiny, polite chuckle. Green eyes twinkled with mirth. Indeed Kana only continued to look and feel just as confused as she did before. "No, I like her. She has spirit. Not many of them have that. I like very much. And Gabriella, you keep this one here." He pointed vaguely at both Kana and Yula. "She will refresh house with her presence."

"Who, me?"

"No. *Sygnomi*, sorry, didn't mean you just then, Kana." Atlas sipped the tea. "Yula Ma Ril. She is of dying race. You humans are destroying rain forest. Eh... all forests. You are clearing out her colony from their homes. Is not your fault; your people, they don't see. But no matter. This one, she is refugee."

"Please, don't fuss over me." Yula fidgeted, rubbed her arms, and stared at the floor. "They can't help it. They don't see us. They forgot all about us. It's just what they do."

But Atlas was relentless.

"Diggers, chainsaws, logging camp, all problems humans cause for Yula's species. Yet she has only love for you and yours, I think. Such a sweet girl. Well worth keeping around. No, as for you Kana," those intimidating eyes swiveled back toward her, putting her in the spotlight again, "you do what you want. You are human after all, you all do what you do, you don't see nobody else anyway. Think you're only ones. You forgot all your old friends. Gods, angels, demons, little peoples, you forget us all. Enlightenment, pah," he scoffed. "Endumb-ne-ment, more like, eh?" He chuckled.

Kana wasn't sure if it was a rant or a joke.

Yula did not thank him for his praise. Instead she curled up tighter into a ball, clearly unhappy with being a subject of his attention. Kana felt a stab at his words too, recoiling, but Gabriella's grip on her tightened. As nonchalant as he behaved, they felt like a scolding. She felt insulted, tossed to one side. As though sensing this, he explained himself.

"I am here only for few days," his tongue clicked, giving his silver head a small shake, "there is no need to feel so hard done by this little talk."

"So you're a mind reader."

The entire room burst into laughter. Even Barney laughed so uproariously, the urge to kick him crossed Kana's mind. "No. Me? No. I am not mind reader. Just old man, maybe. Around long enough to know how you humans think, so easily offended. So personal, all the time. Gabriella, did you not tell her even slightest thing about me?"

"No. Why would I? How often do you make an appearance, once every seventy years? Longer? Why mention you when I didn't expect you? The child has been through enough without, 'oh, by the way, a Titan might show up and would you like another slice of toast, dear?' Really."

Atlas did not grin. "You don't have to be sassy about it."

"Don't I, though? Maybe sassy is the good fit, ah? Maybe I will try it out."

Kana was intrigued, "You're a real Titan?"

Atlas actually grinned, giving her the full power of his omnipotent magnificence in that one charismatic glance. "You felt my presence, yes? Came downstairs, yes?"

"Yes, I did."

"This is ridiculous." Barney scoffed. "What about Yula?"

"Barney" Yula interjected. "It's all fine, really."

"It is not, 'fine', Yula. Ever since the human arrived, she has become the sole topic of conversation."

"And she's not the one doing the talking about her, is she?" Yula folded her arms, giving a dainty pout. "The way I hear it, the poor little thing didn't even want to come here in the first place. She was brought by Chloe. It's the same way the mundanes always end up among us, they get dragged in. You keep saying she's frail and feeble," lovely feminine fingers fluttered toward Kana, "well she is, stuck with you now. Her family is no more friendly than you are, Barney. So stop blaming her for what she didn't and couldn't do about herself. It's tiresome and rude. You're just jealous."

Kana blinked. She had forgotten Yula could be so deep and compassionate, seeing truth in a different light. Maybe Kana was human, but Barney used it like ammunition. Something to be pitied. It didn't sit right. But at least someone else saw how crass it was.

"I am not jealous. I am simply concerned that this fucking conversation has digressed to a jaunty run-around with the lowly pet human who won't even be around one hundred measly years from now."

"You are jealous." Atlas dryly confirmed. Not batting an eye at Barney. "Don't be. If you're right about her, if she is just lowly human like you say, why are you so threatened by her presence here?"

This was out of control. She had to say something. They talked as if she wasn't right here. It was rude. Aside from feeling personally victimised by sullen Barney who was hovering over the salamander, and the excess empathy from Yula, now this Atlas was making comments.

"Look, I am getting sick and fucking tired of this." Kana snapped, rage coiling inside her. She rose to her feet.

Gabriella tugged her back down with a shush. She shrugged her off, anger fueling her bravery enough to be reckless.

"I have a name. Kana. I'm standing right here. Okay, so I can't do all the cute little party tricks you all can, but I'm not worth any less because of it. I'm right here, in the same room with you, and even though I'm not..." she looked about, searching for words, "special like you, I don't belong in the Addams Family. I'm a person with feelings and I deserve some respect."

"Oh dear," Yula's eyes met the floor again.

"Pah." Barney scowled, motioning to leave. Yula squeaked in

protest, pawing at the sleeve of his leather jacket.

"No. Barney. Please stay." She insisted.

There was a grumble, perhaps of protest, but he did as she asked. Arms folded defiantly across his chest. He narrowed his eyes at Kana, "Remember girl, if you disagree with us, you are more than welcome to return to your home, now. Whether in one piece or many."

Gabriella's tongue clicked impatiently against the roof of her mouth, but she held her silence for now.

Kana sat down, her point made.

"Hah." Atlas declared. He frowned into his now empty cup. Bone china? Where did that come from? It looked expensive. "But Kana is not wrong, either. You, Barney. I made you for a purpose. I made you, understand? Kana is a person. You? You are not. You look at her, you see inferior being, which is stupid. She is a superior being. You are idea only," he waggled one finger at Barney as if scolding a child, "she is real person. You keep your mouth," he pinched a beefy thumb and forefinger over his lips. "Like that. Yes?"

Barney didn't answer, but his eyes glared.

"Would you like another cup, Atlas?" Gabriella sweetly asked, rising to her own feet.

"No, is fine. I will make do."

"Of course." Gabriella sat again.

Once again Kana found herself under the full gaze of the Titan, like a royal king waiting for her to speak. "Did you come here because of me?"

"Yes and no. But, eh… mostly no. But now we meet. Troubling times," his tongue clicked, "So now we see." That worried her. Was the Titan judging her, would he make her leave? Everyone else clearly understood his purpose in being here. They were nervous, she could feel it. She hated feeling lost and confused. "Look," Kana dared to express, looking Atlas in the eye as she spoke. "Maybe it's none of my business, but --"

"It isn't." Barney blurted.

"And maybe I don't need to know what's going on," Kana continued.

"You don't." This time, Atlas pointed a finger, but not at her. The line of Barney's lips completely vanished.

He made some shocked noises, but had no mouth to use.

"I told you." The Titan scolded, "Did I not tell you? Don't look mad, you knew I would fix you up if you keep talking. Now I did."

Once again, his gaze settled on the human, giving her his attention.

"But it would be nice nonetheless to be in the loop." Kana shrugged, trying to be diplomatic and polite after her previous outburst. "Whether everybody likes it or not, I live here now, too. I'm part of this household. I know your secrets, about who you are. That makes it my secret, too. I keep my secrets. But it's hard to keep them if I don't know them. So bring me in, all the way. Please? I'm trying really hard to fit in. Don't make me feel like an outsider."

The Spanish woman frowned for a second, eyes darting between Kana and Atlas. Finally, the Titan nodded, giving his permission and Gabriella began to explain.

"You recall Yula unleashing the wrath of fire upon my home? Atlas is here to bind her powers so she might blend easier here while living with me, with us." It made Kana smile that Gabriella included her in that 'us'.

"Will it hurt?" Yula cringed.

"No." Atlas shook his head.

Barney shook his head stubbornly and gestured.

Atlas understood the gestures, "Only because you fought against it, Barney. Binding never hurt those who agree to it."

"Binding?" Kana hinted a question, hoping she might finally get an answer as to who Atlas was. "You tie people up?"

"No, Kana." Gabriella said. "Atlas, *por favor*, shall I tell her?" He gestured a wave by way of consent and she nodded, taking a deep breath to begin. "Atlas is my Master. He helped make me."

"Like, your father?"

A loud snorting noise came from Barney's direction. Gabriella jerked around. "*Perro*." Even Yula let out a tiny giggle. "Atlas found me when I was at my worst. He took me from nothing, saved me."

"I punish you for murderous rampage, Gabriella. Was just. Was right." The Titan firmly corrected.

" You killed someone?" Kana couldn't believe her ears.

Gabriella sighed. "It was a very long time ago."

"But your punishment still stands, girl. Tell her. Confession is good."

Gabriella looked worried, anxious, and uncomfortable. She let out a long sigh. "It was an accident."

"No. It was not accident, you know that." Atlas tick-ticked his tongue as he corrected her. "It was anger. It was revenge."

"It was almost an accident."

"No. You tell all the truth. Raw and real, just like it happen."

Kana tilted her head, wondering what Gabriella could be so anxious about revealing. That first day, Gabriella had come across as dangerous, terrifying even, but now she seemed little more than a beefed up housewife. She clearly had secrets, and Kana was curious.

"I lived in a quiet village many years ago. So long ago, we measured time by the seasons, not calendars. It was a very warm, dry, beautiful country. Often I miss *el sol*, but then I remember how dry and arid the summers were; enough to blister the skin if you stayed out too much in midday. It was me, and *mis hermanos*, my brothers; Francesco, Ricardo, and Eduardo. We lived in our parents home after they had died. We ran a small goat farm, selling milk, cheese, the meat too, to the local people. We did fair."

Kana noted that the more she spoke, the more the Spanish woman wrung her hands, and the more broken her English grew. "My brother, Francesco, he kept holding the farm back, si? He would drink away all our money, claimed it was his money, as the farm is in his name. My other brothers and I, we do not like this, but we have little choice, the farm was in his name. Riccardo, he would often joke that we could kill him and start a fresh. Hide the body somewhere. I liked to continue thinking he was joking, but I am not sure."

Kana nodded as she paused, showing she was listening.

"Every day we wake up early, feed the goats, milk the goats, check and prepare the cheeses, fed the goats again, and bathe them to stop the ticks and the lice, and Francesco, he would watch, make sure we did it right. But sometimes he would not even get out of bed. Sometimes he would tell us we should work harder, he worried so much for our farm, but the more he worries, the more he drinks.'

"So, I think the year was fifteen oh eight when it all changed. I was happy, almost, as best we could be anyway, helping with the farm, working a small garden of food also, I was coming up for thirty and Francesco pulls me aside during our work and says we need to talk about marriage.'

"I should be wedded and a younger man with money has been seen in the village, a proper traveling man and he is looking for a companion. Wants to pay good money instead of asking for a dowry. I tell Francesco, he is not my father. He tells me there is no money to feed me. I bring up the drinking and he beats me for it. No more is said for a while."

Gabriella stared at her hands, continuing, speaking faster.

"My younger brothers, they are more understanding. Riccardo tells me I should marry and bring young sons for the farm. I say I love my home and my work with the goats. Eduardo and Riccardo talk no more of it. I think perhaps Francesco talked with them.'

"The next day the young man is brought up to the farm to see me. He is buying me, Francesco tells me, so I must be pretty, I must look *muy bonita*. I am put in a dress, made to stand in a *dulce* way, be polite and talk of only girl things. It is not me, I tell him, and he beats me for talk back. But not my face, because he needs me pretty; I think he was very drunk that day. More violent."

Gabriella stopped her tirade of fast, frenzied, Spanish tinted words, looking across the room into the middle distance. Her tongue clicked against the roof of her mouth. Amber eyes narrowed, and finally blinked. She pressed her lips tight. None of the others spoke. Not even Barney, who was staring out of the window with a faraway look in his own eyes too. Yula was curled up, rocking back and forth.

Kana, however, had yet to get her mind pass the year "fifteen oh eight." While she understood Gabriella has the ability to return to life from death, and had just about come to terms with it, she had not realised that Gabriella could be so old. The immortal woman was over five centuries old. "Of course, the man came to the farm. He looks at me, sleazy, I do not like him. He was an arrogant *perro*, thinks he is important. Of course, I slap him." Gabriella's eyes turn to Kana, watching her reaction.

"He bends me over *la mesa*; I already buy you, he yells, you will marry me. Again, I refuse as he continues. Francesco lets him. When he finally leaves, Francesco beats me again. Grabs the poker for the fire and cold metal,"The Spanish woman frowns, her face hardening. The thin white line of that diagonal scar shines in the light and she drags her fingertip along it. "If I don' want to marry, I don' need be pretty, he says. I need to learn my place and Riccardo comes in. My brothers fight and Riccardo says he has gone too far.'

"I am crying on the floor, *bella* dress all ripped, there is blood on me and my dress, and my brother's nose bleeds too. The next day I run away." Gabriella's face softened to a weary frown now, eyes moist as they remain on Kana. Atlas prompted her on with a roll of his hand. "I do not know how far I run, but I wore only the clothes on my back. No spare. No food, no shoes. *Dios mío,* I walked for three days before I faint, too weak to stand. There is a small cave, away from the heat and sun. I crawl inside. I sleep."

Gabriella's eyes closed, recalling the memory. "Everything hurts, when I wake. I think I might die, the soil is almost wet, like little sand under my fingers. I can feel death's kiss on my body."

Barney gave a dry purr. Kana noted that his mouth had been returned to him and his own eyes were shut too. "I remember this, Gabriella." He finally speaks, "you were so weak then. Beautiful. Tiny, frightened little bird, but now you are strong. You could have been mine."

Gabriella gave a tiny hiccough of a laugh, wiped her eyes, and opened them.

"I'm stronger for beating you."

"What happened, Gabriella?" Kana burst. "Death spoke to me. He told me not to drink from the wet sandy soil. My mouth is so dry, so I dig at the cool wet soil, the water pools and I drink. I scratch on, drink the muddy water."

"You defied me." Barney growled. "I told you not to drink the water, and now I can't touch you."

"Water," Kana was confused. "He can't touch you because of water?"

"*El agua de Vida.*" Gabriella trilled. "The fountain of youth, whatever you call it. I found it. *Por la gracia de Dios*, I found it."

"I discovered I could not die when I lay there for three more days without dying." Gabriella held up three fingers. "Without nothing but the water. I healed, my face healed, my body; so I go home."

"And?" Atlas prompted.

"Short story, I stabbed the fire poker through Francesco's throat when he slept. Riccardo tries to stop me, " Her voice faltered. Her jaw set. "I did not learn my full strength. I killed Riccardo and Eduardo ran into the village they all came after me. First few, then many. Monstruo, monstruo they all shouted and they burned me. They tie me to a wooden board, burn me for a witch and when there was nothing left for burning, I healed. Death wouldn't have me. For hours I screamed." Gabriella was shaking now , her fingers biting into the leather of the couch. Her voice snapping angrily, "Screaming because you humans always kill the things you don't want to know about, the things you fear. "

"I warned you not to drink it." Barney reminded. "You didn't listen."

"When I came back, they burned me again. Tried to drown me. Pulled me down with stones and rope. I was so. angry." Indeed Gabriella seemed to be angry now. Icicles were growing from her fingernails, crackling against the leather of the couch. Her hair was glossy with growing flecks of ice. "So I burned them."

Kana didn't say a word. Her voice was frozen in her throat. After being subjected to everything, Gabriella had finally snapped and turned upon the people in her village. Her friends, her family, she lost everything, but gained immortality.

"I was alone then, the only one of my village to be alive after the burning. They deserved it. "

"Enough." Atlas growled, his voice was quiet with authority. Everyone, including Barney stiffened, turning away from Gabriella. A heavy dread and fear churned through Kana. "It was fire like from Bible, Gabriella. Everybody comes, everybody say, 'look'. Everybody wants to know, 'Will you do something?' So I go to her town, I find her." Atlas explains to Kana, "When super natural creatures threaten balance, nature calls to me. I'm supposed to put it back on level, understand? I have to destroy her. I don't want to."

"He found me, shaking and crying like a pitiful bebé. He took me in. Cared for me"

"Until you run away, you tart." But he gave a light laugh, proving he wasn't angry. "Yes, I care; you run away. But that was not issue.

You were stable then. You could look after yourself."

"Where does Barney come into this?" Kana was in awe. Gabriella's story sounded completely unbelievable, but she continued to listen, eager for more.

"I wanted more company." Gabriella grinned. "Atlas fashioned me a friend out of my Death, and here he stands. A good friend."

"Ah, but Gabriella had lesson to learn." Atlas mused, the wisdom shining in his eyes. "She did not want marriage so badly, it resulted in destroying her loved ones, yes? I had to see to it that she could not do, eh moisty dance with her new friend, yes? Her suffering is hers alone."

"So, that's, why Barney can't touch anyone," Yula chirped in, breaking her silence.

Atlas gave a smile and nodded.

"I keep world in balance. Vincent's lycanthropy too violent, so violent." Named and pointed, proving the wise Titan was aware the werewolf was upstairs. "So I give him little control. Chloe's blood was too powerful, so I make it taste sour for humans, yes? These other vampires, their blood is so mmm. Yum. Is not good.. Lola, well, she is just child, and so I only forbid her ability to change into dangerous things. No creature big enough to hurt a person should have soul of person, yes? Reasonable, I think. Child still maintains her freedom. I don't have to worry about dragon again."

Kana did not inquire about the dragon.

"Wait," She had another, more important question. "If you didn't want Gabriella to have a baby, how did Lola," She worded things carefully, not intending to let Gabriella know what Barney had told her.

"I am sometimes busy." Atlas glared at Gabriella. "Not always am I watching. I do not well with the micromanaging."

Gabriella did not bother to hide her smirk. "And yet, here I stand without a wedding ring," she purred, content.

"Mmm, so it is." Amused, the corner of his mouth twitched upward. "As for Yula, I will take only fire."

"No." Yula was on her feet in seconds. "Oh please. No, you can't. I won't let it happen again, please, you can't. It's all I have left. -"

"Pretty little one, I have to. You destroy kitchen. Nature calls me.

Anyway, is overdue, yes? For giving fire to the humans, you knew we did not want them to have."

"Forgive me, Atlas." Barney was behind her in seconds. Leather-clad hand on the red-head's shoulder. She shook, before burying herself in Barney's chest, sobbing. "But that is excessive. She needs her fire her spark."

"Her immunity to flame, that she will keep. Her hands, her mind she will still shape fire. But while she is here, there will be no" he seemed to reach for the words, "no bringing the fire ex nihilo, from nowhere; summoning. She will not summon flame. I think Gabriella, you make a room with a heater, yes?"

"Atlas," Barney leered, stepping forward to challenge him. Atlas merely pointed; Barney slumped back into his chair as though he were a marionette whose strings had just been cut.

"I made you, son." Atlas said quietly. "Unmaking you would not be more difficult." The bearded man tapped a large fingertip against a curly-haired temple. "You keep that in your mind, yes? You do not stand up at me like that again, yes?" The resulting look on Barney's face had Kana recoil into the back of the chair. She frowned, considering all she had heard. Poor Gabriella. There was a new found respect for the woman in the back of her heart.

" But what about," She interjected and blue eyes meeting his omnipotent green once more. "But you didn't explain the ice thing. Gabriella has ice, not fire; you gave her that power, right?"

"Oh," Atlas turned, sneered, and yet he gave the most docile of laughs. "Merely delicious irony on my part. I couldn't quite resist."

"I killed mis hermanos. I killed mis amigos. En incendio," Gabriella added, "and he think it is hilarious to give me ice."

"I had to cool fiery core of yours somehow, *Koukla mou*." As Atlas rose to his feet, he bid them good day. "For now, I will find room. Yula, I will give you day to come to terms with it. Try not to burn down anything in meantime, eh? I know you are good girl, so sweet. You don't want to hurt anyone. Is for best."

This did not seem fair on Yula. She l had been terrified, worried that Gabriella had died touching Barney. Sure Barney was intolerable, unpleasant, slimy, and repulsed Kana, but then, if he was Death incarnate, surely he was supposed to, she reasoned. "If Yula is a salamander," she asked, as politely as she could, "and her kind gave human fire, and Gabriella burned down the human village; aren't you kinda punishing her for what Gabriella did?"

"Please," Yula tried to bargain too, her face finally appearing from the sanctuary of Barney's leather clad midriff. Black tears rolled down her face. Like oil. "I need my fire."

Atlas' smile at Kana turned to a frown, his eyes narrowing. "Do not question me, child. You see what she do to kitchen. If fear does that to her, then all human civilization is at threat with her living in your town. Gabriella is consequence of her family's gift. I am old man; not so old as some, but I am here. There is problem? I fix. Is no bad thing for Yula. World is changing. World keeps moving, rolling on, on, on. Time for Yula catch up."

With that, Atlas was done talking about it. He swept from the room and headed along the corridor to one of the few ground floor rooms. Near the end, he turned. "Gabriella, you have good people. Strong people. They look out for each other, that is family. Is good."

Gabriella let out a long sigh, leaning forward to rest her head in her hands. Her body hunched up. Kana stood up.

"How could you let him get away with that?" She asked, incredulous. "Gabriella, how the hell couldn't you have made him see reason?"

"It doesn't work like that. Atlas isn't a person, any more than Barney is. But what Atlas is; he's balance. He works on reason and logic, not emotional manipulation."

"If you weren't here in the first place, this may not have happened." Barney snarled, wrapping his arms further around the distraught salamander who only cried harder at Kana's words.

"Fuck you." Kana snapped.

"Shut up, Barney." Gabriella said weakly through her hands. "It has nothing to do with Kana and you know it. Leave her out of it. And Kana, be quiet."

"Oh yes, defend the human, how admirable of you Gabriella. Like your Master, you always take the side of the pathetic mortals." Barney hissed back. "Please do tell, in which way, shape, or form, that you're going to blame yourself for what just happened this time?"

"You know what, Barney?" Gabriella's face finally left her hands.

"I have had half again enough of your shit, your pathetic."

"Stop it." Yula pitched in. "Please stop shouting at each other."

Kana kept quiet. There was nothing she could say to alleviate the situation. Atlas disregarded her plea for Yula.

Gabriella gave another deep sigh and stood. "Who wants hot chocolate?"

Kana gave a nod, feeling her heart sink. Gabriella sounded exhausted. Yula sniffed and nodded. Gabriella stalked into the nearest bathroom where the kettle had been plugged in, since the kitchen was inoperable. Kana was quick to follow, not keen on spending time with Barney without the Spanish woman as a buffer.

The woman muttered to herself in a quiet, frantic Spanish under her breath as she flicked down the switch on the kettle. She barely noticed Kana had followed until she turned, almost crashing into her.

"Ay. Kana. *Qué estás haciendo?* What are you doing? You almost gave me a heart attack."

"Well, at least you wouldn't have died from it." Kana gave a nervous chuckle.

Gabriella raised an eyebrow, not amused.

"Be careful around Atlas. He's usually a sweet old man, but sometimes he is not." Gabriella explained pulling mugs from the medicine cabinet.

Kana rubbed her arms. "Is he always so right?"

"Si." Gabriella nodded. "You get used to his way. He is looking out for your kind after all."

"But Yula needs her fire, doesn't she?"

"Si," Gabriella nodded, playing with the mug in her hand. "Si, she does, but we can keep the house warm for her. Heaters in her room, extra blankets. I will not turn her out simply because of a few extra needs for her survival. This is a safe house, after all. To give aid and comfort where I can; that's why this house is here."

"It's good, what you do."

Gabriella sighed. "I just want a happy quiet house; a place where I can look after each other and be safe, live quietly, and help out those that need a place to go. Is that hard? No, but Atlas here complicates things. I do not want for her to leave, even though that is ultimately her choice. I expect she might if it means losing her fire, but it is her choice. Barney will be not happy."

"Barney's never happy. Wait. What?" Kana's eyes widened, "You mean those two are dating now? How on earth would that work? He can't touch anyone."

Gabriella burst into a trill of laughter, looked ashamed at herself, and then grinned. "I do not want to think about that. What he does is his business."

"True," she completely agreed. "Hey, Gabriella?"

"Si?"

"I'm sorry for what those people did to you. I don't think all people would have wanted to burn you."

Gabriella said nothing, busying herself with the hot kettle, pouring the scalding water into the three mugs and spooning in the cocoa. "Do not take mind of that, Kana. Maybe it was your ancestors, but maybe not. That doesn't matter. *You* are not your ancestors. You are only you. Here." She handed the young woman a mug. "Drink up."

Kana gave a nod, taking a tiny sip of the burning hot liquid. Thick, the hot cocoa lined her throat in a pleasant, comforting way.

13

Still reeling from Atlas, Kana did not expect that there would be another visitor to the hotel so soon. After Gabriella left Atlas to settle on a room and those still downstairs drank their hot cocoa, the house descended into an uneasy silence until the front door swung open yet again.

"Oh, what now?" Barney complained.

The figure in the hallway stood tall and straight. His glacier blue eyes swept the foyer with a slight interest, his thumb and forefinger curling across his chin and he swung the door closed without a backward glance.

He looked like a biker. Black leather trousers tucked into engineer boots seemed to complete the ensemble that led up to a black and jade leather motorcycle jacket. Dark hair. Under his arm, the man cradled a gold coloured motorcycle helmet that sported a lacquered illustration of ram's horns along the sides.

The corners of his lips twitched up into a devilish smirk; icy blue eyes met Kana's own. That finger straightened and pressed against his lips, silently suggesting silence, as if he himself was some awful secret.

Kana watched him with curious fascination. He moved with an artful grace, somehow quick and yet smooth at once, ran his fingers along the wall as he passed into the living room.

Something about him screamed for her attention.

"Oh, look -- a whole menagerie of the bizarre. How cute." When he finally spoke, his voice was deep and smooth, with a purr in it. Kana detected Norwegian in his accent. "You can all relax about the policemen who were skulking around outside. I've sent them off chasing a squirrel."

His eyebrows lifted in a falsified pride upon his face, like some proud mother cat surveying her kittens.

Barney looked at him coldly. Even Yula glanced up from her hiding spot between his arms.

"If you seek a room, wait for Gabriella to return." Barney growled, clearly still aggravated by Atlas. "Sit down and take a number."

The stranger's lips parted into a Cheshire cat's grin of teeth somehow seeming sharp in their brightness. He tutted. "No." The swiftness with which the stranger covered the space between himself and Barney startled Kana. "That's not how this works. Not with me."

What is this one? Kana's heart thundered. He did not seem entirely stable.

His next move was no less startling. He reached out and with superhuman grace plucked the leather glove from Barney's left hand and threw it to the floor. He seized the taller man's wrist, and wrenched it up to the height of his chin. He looked at no one except Barney, not even the tiny Salamander curled in his lap.

"Notice what's not happening." His voice came softly.. "Notice what you can't do to me. Think about what that means. Now, behave yourself, or I'll show you what I can do."

Barney's face paled, his nostrils flared, and yet he urged Yula from his lap. The Salamander frowned, looked uneasy as always, and fluttered to the other side of the room, half hiding behind Kana.

Apparently there would be no solving this without a fight.

The stranger blinked, seemingly amused as Barney rose to his feet. The shade of death had two inches on the raven haired stranger, who didn't seem bothered in the slightest. He glanced up, meeting his green eyes and stretched, long and languid, his arms rising up over his head. When they returned back down the stranger met Barney for height, almost looming over him.

Barney growled and took a step back.

"What is this power?"

"Power?" The stranger's hand reached up to his chest in a flamboyant display of offence. "You know nothing of power." He turned his back on Barney and headed towards Kana.

"*Raring*," The stranger spoke to Kana in Swedish. The word for "darling". His smile was so full of sweetness. Kana had to take a step back, almost knocking over Yula who clung to her like a lost puppy. "Perhaps you can tell me where this Gabriella is, hmm? I should like to see the rooms."

Kana opened her mouth but before anything Barney roared at the stranger.

"Enough. She's just a human.." He spluttered and stormed towards the raven haired newcomer.

With a mere sigh and a heavy roll of his eyes the stranger turned. He merely pointed a finger, but at the gesture, Barney flew off his feet, backward.

"Didn't I tell you to behave?" the stranger asked with an amused lift of one eyebrow. He padded over to the fallen man like a house cat grinning its way toward a crippled mouse. He leaned down, canted his head slightly, and asked, "Are we learning yet?"

He straightened, looked around the room. "Well, this is turning out to be an amusing little house, isn't it?"

Barney staggered up, braced against the kitchen wall, and Yula ran to him, muttering a warning. The stranger shook his head and waggled his finger with a nose scrunching grin.

"No, my dear. That youngster got bratty and has been corrected. Don't undo my good work, now. I'm not here to cause fights or fuss, but I won't be mouthed off to by a toddler." A faint growl rumbled down the staircase followed by the wolf man himself who had finally decided to join them. No doubt roused by the drama occurring downstairs. Vincent eyed the stranger and pulled a look of sheer disgust.

"Oh, stop showing off, old man."

"Mind your tone, son." the stranger grinned. "You're not so big I can't put you over my knee as well. Now," he turned his ice-blue gaze on Kana, "will you call Gabriella for me?"

Kana hollered out the Spanish woman's name as loud as she could possibly muster.

"Kana." Gabriella thundered back as she descended the stairs, regarding the brunette with a dour look. "Really? Is there any need for that? Oh. Hola. " Gabriella blinked, seeing Barney's pale demeanour and the stranger in her hallway.

"I'm afraid there's been a bit of a misunderstanding." The stranger announced, shaking his head. "Your friend decided to be unwelcoming. He had to be corrected. I'd like a room."

"I know who you are." Gabriella replied warily, still watching Barney and clearly trying to decipher what had transpired. "You're not welcome here."

"Oh, I know." The man flashed that Cheshire grin. "I'm not welcome anywhere." He advanced toward the staircase, prompting Gabriella to take two steps up and back. "Nevertheless, I'm staying, for a short time, at any rate. Let's make that as painless as possible, shall we?"

"Upstairs room or downstairs?" Gabriella asked, her unhappiness written on her face.

"Downstairs, I think. What are your rates? I know I'm not wanted here, so I do expect you to be ridiculous about the price. Not that it matters."

Gabriella nodded, her arms folded and her hip canted to one side. "Ridiculous? That can be arranged. Five hundred a night. How's that? Ridiculous enough for you?"

The stranger nodded, then looked at Kana. She blushed. He winked. "I'll give you a thousand a night. I may have to be particularly loathsome. But let's pray not."

Gabriella blinked rapidly. "Let's go look."

That Gabriella, normally unflappable, was clearly put so off her ease by this stranger sent goosebumps rising on Kana's skin.

After the two had receded into the hallway, Kana returned to the living room. Everyone sat around the room looking uncomfortable.

"Okay, who or *what* was that?" Kana demanded. Even Barney looked like he had a mouthful of lemon juice. No one spoke up. "Well?" After another sombre moment, Vincent answered. "That, lass, was the prince of lies."

"Yeah, okay." Kana snorted. "That guy is the Devil?" That seemed a bridge too far for her to cross.

"Worse." Even little Yula, usually so ebullient, sounded timid. "The Twister. The shaper of nightmares. "

"Oh, stop it." Vincent growled. "You talk about him like he's the worst thing ever. He's just playful."

"He plays with reality itself." Barney seethed. "He is a perpetual menace toying with reality like a child with a rattle."

"And how is that different from Atlas?" Vincent shot back. "You're living because of that kind of power. Don't you sit there and mouth off about it."

Barney stood so fast he sent his chair backward. "I grow weary of that kind of power and of sitting down. You say one more word to me and I will … "

"Shut up!" Kana shouted. She shook her head vehemently and stomped her foot down hard. Her finger pointed at Barney, and if the finger trembled, she neither noticed nor cared. "You pompous, cantankerous swine. Since I got here it's oh, puny human this, pathetic mortal that. Now you're the one being scraped off somebody's shoes like dirt and you whine like a bitch! Well boo fucking hoo. Just shut the hell up."

She stormed from the room.

Vincent watched her go, then looked to the glowering Barney, then the shocked face of Yula, then the bearded face of Atlas, who popped into the living room and asked, "Did I miss something exciting?"

14

It wasn't until hunger panged in her stomach that Kana dragged herself from her room to make her discomfort known. She stared longingly into the kitchen, wishing for a miracle. The smell of mildew and damp had reached a level where entering the kitchen without a mask seemed impossible. She wrinkled her nose.

"Bad business, this. Unsightly." That dark haired stranger waltzed in from behind her and twirled around the kitchen, taking in the state of disarray. "How can a person of taste and distinction be expected to live in a house with this for a scullery, I ask you. No, I don't find this satisfactory, not at all."

He leant back against the lopsided table and snapped his fingers.

The kitchen appeared to blur along the edges. All manner of objects zipped across the room, blending into each other, diverging, and ran apart. Kana felt disorientated watching; as though staring into a hidden picture image. By the time everything settled, the kitchen looked almost as good as new.

Almost. Kana couldn't figure out what, but something was odd about it. Odd enough to cause concern.

"Well, now." The unwelcome guest clapped his hands together, rubbing them as he beamed his shark-like grin around the kitchen, and sat down in one of the renewed chairs. "Isn't this much better?. We can bring the kettle back through now. Girl, be a dear little creature and fetch me coffee."

Kana frowned. She didn't think it wise to disobey him, but she would not play maid for him.

He leaned back slightly, eyebrows lifting. "Faster would be better. You wouldn't want me to get restless from waiting. I might decide you look better as another animal, just to keep myself entertained. Actually," he leaned towards her and peered over bridged fingers, his elbows gracing the table. "Have you ever considered the zebra? It's a horse, but with style. The tiger of horses. You'd make a fine zebra, girl." His grin brought Kana's cheeks out in colour.

"Who are you?" She fumbled out the words, flustered by what she supposed to be a compliment. "What are you? And why are you here?"

"So many questions," he tutted. "Run along and fetch the kettle, make me coffee, and perhaps – just perhaps – I'll humour you with answers."

Kana reluctantly agreed, heading towards the bathroom to fetch cups, the kettle and the milk from the bath tub. She couldn't deny that freezing the water in the bathtub to keep things fresh had been a genius idea.

"Now there's a good pet. Put everything on the counter top and make the coffee well. Favour me with a question."

"Um questions." Kana returned his Cheshire Cat grin with her best approximation, then plugged the kettle in, filled it, and set it to boil. Looking around for coffee, she almost knocked over a jar of it that she swore she hadn't picked up from the bathroom. "Alright, your name. What's your name?"

"Oh, but I have so many."

Kana waited for him to clarify but it appeared that was all he would give her. "Such as?"

"That depends on who you ask." He gave her the most patently fake innocent expression she'd ever seen. Kana almost swore.

"And how many people call you Dirty Son Of A --"

"Ah." The stranger raised a finger, waved it gently and tutted. "Let's not be uncivil. It might become a contest, and I fear you wouldn't like my competitive spirit. And don't neglect the coffee."

Kana formulated something good and stinging, when he twirled that upraised finger and she twirled with it, turning to face the mug of instant coffee.

"Luca Faesson. Please, if you must stay, can I ask you not to bother my guests too much?" Gabriella stormed into the kitchen. "Though I must admit I am grateful for the renovation."

"Of course." The raven haired one nodded his head in gentle understanding. "I am too kind, am I not? To fix your kitchen, I would say I deserve compensation. Perhaps in the form of one who take a little less goading to make coffee. Your pet is not well trained."

Kana opened her mouth and Gabriella swiftly covered it with her hand.

"She will learn in time, Luca. For now I shall make it." She ushered Kana to the other side of the kitchen. Kana felt like she'd missed something. To herself, Gabriella chuckled darkly and muttered. "Compensation. For a cheap parlour trick."

If Luca heard his host's comment, he gave no sign of it. "It pleases me to see that someone here knows how to do things properly." Luca turned to face Kana and nodded. "You may entertain me with another question." He crossed one leg across the other, his raised foot slowly beginning to twirl.

"Why are --"

"Luca, is my floor on the ceiling?"

"Oh, that's?" Luca cast a bemused glance upward, then leaned in his chair and took in the ceiling. "Hmm." Kana did a double take. Linoleum tiles above, painted alabaster below. It unsettled her.

After a moment, Luca shrugged. "I like them better this way. Human ceilings are usually so uninteresting. And unless you drop something, what cause have you to ever lay eyes on your floor?"

"Madre de Dio" Kana heard a tiny whine from the Spanish woman who promptly finished preparing the coffee. "Now you have coffee. I would prefer it if you returned to your room."

Luca sipped the coffee. "Gabriella, what in that room could possibly entertain me?"

"Read a book."

He smirked. "You know, manhood might have suited you better. Have you tried it? Or wait -- are you trying it, now?"

Gabriella set her jaw. "The only extra pene in my house today is you."

Kana snorted out a laugh, despite how hard she tried to hide it behind wide eyes and her hand. The Spanish woman flashed a glare at her and she immediately glanced away.

"Don't even think of doing it, Luca. Don't. You. Dare." Gabriella growled, but there was clear panic in her body language.

"Oh, you're no fun." Luca sulked. Then just as quickly as he'd pouted, he threw a grin back at Kana, clearly considering something unfathomable. "Perhaps bigger assets then."

Kana knew exactly what he had planned even before the first two buttons on Gabriella's shirt popped. Both the women's faces reddened.

"Desist. Please, there is no need for --"

"Christ on a bike." Vincent blinked, wandering into the kitchen with the biggest grin that any human male could possibly possess. "Must say, I fancy the new look, Gabby."

There was little for Gabriella to do but storm out of the kitchen in embarrassment, aiming a slap in Vincent's direction as she passed. Clearly distracted, the slap missed; Vincent jerked back from it easily.

"Tsk. You'd think she'd be grateful. How many girls go under primitive surgeons' knives for pathetic copies of what I can give quickly and freely?" He glanced at Kana and held out his hand. "This one for example."

Kana folded her arms.

"Y'know," Vince said gruffly, peering into the newly repaired fridge at though it might, by some sheer coincidence contain food. "I liked her better as she was. But the kitchen looks much better. Not sure about the floor."

"You'll learn to love it, Ulf."

"Wow, wait, you can change anything and everything? Just like that?"

"Not precisely the way you mean. But is the room not tolerable now? Is the air not less offensive?" Luca rolled his eyes and waved her question away as though it were mediocre and pointless. "Must you find fault?"

"So, you could give Barney a donkey's head? Just the head?"

"If it would amuse me. And now that you've suggested it."

"Kana, don't tempt fate. Or Luca." Vincent warned. Luca beamed in his direction. "You're gonna sort Gabby out, right?"

Luca's grin melted away until he pouted. "Nothing but complaints do I get for my generosity. I could have stayed home for this kind of treatment."

"Luca." Barney roared from somewhere. Luca did not move, unperturbed. Vincent backed up, pulling an arm around Kana and tugging her towards the back door, newly refitted into its hinges

With a wave of his hand, Luca and coffee disappeared just as the shade entered the kitchen. Kana's thoughts spun. Vincent shook his head and grunted out a chuckle.

"He was here, wasn't he." Barney snarled. "What has he done to Gabriella? She stormed upstairs in utter mortification."

Kana and Vincent looked around, neither of them willing or able to tell him. Neither could keep a straight face. Luca waltzed in through the kitchen door behind Barney and leaned over his shoulder, behaving as if he just arrived. His left arm curled around Barney's neck and he sipped his coffee around the shade.

"So easily shape-able, that one, isn't she?" He pressed himself flush to Barney, who growled, clearly uncomfortable with the Trickster's arm so close to his throat. "You know, I have a marvelous idea. Kana, how would you like to borrow a power? Wouldn't that be a riot, Barney?" He nuzzled his head against Barney. The shade did not turn, but instead his shoulders rose and fell in barely contained rage.

"You don't much care for me, do you, Barnabus?" Luca cooed. He turned his face, those blue eyes were still on Kana, and whispered in the taller being's ear, "Count your blessings I'm only having a holiday." He turned his face fully back to Kana. "Now then, little human, what is the word?"

Kana almost jumped at the idea. Her eyes lighting up but Vincent shot her a look.

"Careful, lass. Make it airtight first." He warned. "What's the catch?"

"Catch?" Luca raised his hand in faux umbrage, finally releasing Barney, who stalked away from him with a snarl. Luca chuckled and found his seat. "Oh, I would never oh, maybe I would. But no, not this time. Consider it a gift."

"Why?" Kana narrowed her eyes.

"How predictably dull. Because the misanthrope there hates humans and suddenly you won't strictly be one anymore. I mean to rob him of his excuse to antagonize you, which will only make him more antagonistic toward you."

"So just to take the piss out of him," Kana nodded towards Barney.

Luca burst into raucous laughter.

Barney visibly seethed.

After a moment, the trickster slapped his thigh. "In point of fact, yes, that cuts right to the heart of it. But also, now as my way of saying thank you for that."

Kana looked at Vincent. The wolf man shrugged, scratching his head.

"All right," Kana relented. "What kind of power?"

"There are only two rules -- no, sorry three. You get only one gift. It cannot be omnipotence. Finally, it must be something fun." Luca sat up and leant towards her, the leather of his outfit creaking as he moved. "Go on, suggest something."

Kana paused. Fun? She glanced around her.

"Flying?"

Luca laughed at her.

"Alright, the What about --"

"For the love of God, do not suggest shape-shifting. This house already has one too many shifters now." Vincent grumbled.

Luca shot him a smug grin full of pearly white teeth.

"My dear, how about something a little baser? Then perhaps you can thank me with it as you test it?" He spread his legs as he spoke, by an un-gentlemanly amount.

Kana's eyes grew wide again.

"No." Vincent announced, somewhat loudly.

"I want to manipulate things too." She had to think. Not fire, Yula had fire and Atlas was here to stop that. Perhaps ice. Ice could form pretty crystals. Perhaps she could make ice sculptures. "Ice. I want ice powers."

"Oh, that's almost too easy. Are you sure you don't hunger for something with a little more zest?"

Vincent shook his head in warning.

"Like?" Kana asked, intrigued.

"What about turning people into frogs? That one's useful and fun. Mmm on second thought no. Humans might still do the whole witch burning thing. What about transforming yourself into an animal?

"No shape-shifting."

"Hush, Ulf. Wouldn't you like to be a little dainty unicorn?"

"What's with you and horses?" Vincent growled.

Luca tapped his nose and frowned. "Didn't I just tell you to hush? Don't make me muzzle you."

"I want ice." Kana insisted.

Luca sighed and waved his hand. Barney, still lurking in the corner, pressed himself against the wall as though anticipating chaos.

"Done, and done." Luca yawned. "Well? Let 'er rip, as they say."

"Careful lass." Vincent urged again. "Be very careful."

Kana held out her hands, curious to see if anything would happen. She focused, wondering how this would work, and turned her hands sideways. The lightbulb above her popped and she squealed, jumping back.

Luca looked up, then at Kana and scratched the back of his head absent-mindedly.

"That did not appear to be ice. I may be a touch rusty at this. Terrible shame." The look of smug superiority on his face betrayed a lie.

Barney and Vincent shook their heads.

"Luca, take it back. This is not a good idea."

"Isn't it?" The Trickster sipped his coffee again and paused, pulling out a shard of the bulb from it and flicking it to the floor. "Oh, but this is fun."

"I don't like it." Kana exclaimed, lowering her hands slowly. The cup in Luca's hands splintered, coffee spilled everywhere. She squealed louder, looking worried.

"Pity I was just beginning to like that coffee." He conjured a towel from nowhere and wiped down his leather attire, but not the table. "But it is amusing."

"Kana just keep still." Vincent suggested grabbing her wrists. "Barney, get Gabriella or Atlas. Hell, get both."

Barney shook his head. "The human encouraged him. It's her own fault."

Vincent took a deep breath. "Just don't move, Kana."

"Okay."

Vincent ran upstairs to fetch someone and Kana froze on the spot. Luca grinned and glided over. Barney, seemingly helpless, watched in discomfort from the doorway going to the living room.

"Tell me, girl, tell me true; are you ticklish?"

Kana shook her head and backed up, her hands remaining at her sides. "Don't. No. Don't touch me."

Luca gave her a patronizing look. "Do you really think I have to *touch* you to tickle you?"

"Don't," She whispered.

Luca shrugged. "Very well. I won't tickle you at all." Instead, he merely looked down at her belly, at her shirt, and something slithered along Kana's spine. Her body jerked, trying not to itch.

"What is that?." She screamed, the weight of something living winding around her underneath her clothing.

"A pet for the pet; a serpent from the serpent," Luca chuckled, enjoying her discomfort. "Do you not like him? He won't bite, but it'd be a shame if you blasted half your own body and destroyed the house while trying to evict him."

"I don't like snakes." Kana whimpered and squirmed. Even Barney had an awkward mixture of amusement and horror on his face. Her body jerked again, as the creature slithered around her waist. She could feel every inch of it and fought a sob. "I don't like it."

"Is it the scales? Perhaps,-" Another subtle gesture of his hand and the smooth touch of the skin turned bristly. Soft, yet uncomfortable. Kana yelped and threw her arms up.

"Feathers?." She squealed before several of the kitchen cupboards exploded from the wall. Luca laughed riotously and clapped his hands.

Barney growled.

"Luca this is enough." Even the spectral misanthrope had seen as much as he cared to.

"You are, all of you, boring." Luca sneered, but he did nothing, despite Kana's violent squirming.

"Get rid of it." Kana squealed again, the urge to itch so overpowered her that she ground her teeth audibly. "Please. Ah, this is awful."

She yelped and winced as the feathered creature slithered up between her breasts and around her throat. Her arms flew to her throat. The creature exploded in a blood red fountain that sent sinew and tissue everywhere, but mostly all over the inside of her clothing. A full-body shudder of disgust shook her from head to toe. She could feel the bile rise in her gut and fought the urge to vomit.

"Oh God."

"Now that was entertainment." Luca declared just as both Atlas and Gabriella appeared, Vincent close behind them.

"Luca, what are you doing?" Gabriella demanded as she finished buttoning a new, larger shirt. Atlas shot Luca a look that demanded an explanation.

"S-snake." Kana managed. She hadn't moved from her stiff position in the corner.

"Fix it. Now. Luca." Atlas growled.

Luca looked offended. "What makes you think it was me?"

"Right Now." Atlas repeated.

Luca gave a small sigh, and did as he was told. The feathers, tissue and other remnants glowed, flared as if sunlight passed over them, and disappeared from Kana and inside her clothing. She slapped and brushed at herself with furious abandon. The same passing sun fire passed over the kitchen. When it faded, the room was the burnt shambles it had been the day before.

"I need a shower," Kana failed to even notice the change in her surroundings, the thought of even having a snake touch her enough to cause discomfort.

Vincent ushered her through the door into the living room and whispered close to her ear. "It was just an illusion. I'm sorry. I should have spoken up sooner when he offered you a gift. I would have if I'd known he was going to take you on a bad trip. But Kana, none of these things can really hurt you."

"But it felt so real," Kana rubbed away the goosebumps on her skin.

"The mind feels what it's tricked to feel. He's a trickster, a fiend, and a royal mind-fuck, but I'm certain Atlas will know how to deal with him. Hopefully before things go too out of hand."

"But my hands moved and things exploded." Kana insisted.

"His timing is impeccable." Vincent sighed. "It all just a very grand and awful magic show. He's basically harmless. He's just looking for a rise. Listen to me, because this is very important: if you play along, he'll upset you. And if you get upset, you give him what he wants. And if you give him what he wants, he won't be satisfied. He's never satisfied, he just keeps pulling the string for more. Understand? You cannot give him what he wants by getting upset." Kana didn't imagine that would be easy but she nodded. She peered back into the kitchen, finally noticing the wreck it had reverted to.

Maybe a shower could wait.

Together, the returned to the rest of the group.

Atlas did not look pleased and for the first time she was glad the Titan had appeared. Perhaps he could control Luca.

"Why don't we all just calm down and have something to drink. Barney, would you care to share that exquisite whiskey you have hiding in the cupboard up there?" Gabriella narrowed her eyes but motioned for Barney to agree.

The shade growled low but fetched it and begrudgingly passed it to Luca.

"Kana, was it? Come here, sweetheart."

Kana shot him a venomous look that caused his smile to fade. He patted his lap. While he did look genuinely sorry, Kana chose not to sit. Vincent had advised her not to play along, but she worried. What if that would only make him try harder?

"I only meant to entertain, provide a bit of fun. I did not intend to cause you such offence and discomfort," he said, peering up through his lashes. Kana wondered what had been said in her absence. "Will you forgive me? A drink to our good health, hmm?"

He un-stoppered the bottle and took a long swig, enough to invoke a snort of air from Barney. Kana hesitated as he thrust it out melodramatically towards her. Nobody moved save Luca, whose head tilted slightly. His lip wobbled.

He couldn't hide the guilt on his face, she realised; she reached out for the bottle. It exploded before she could grab it. She screamed and leapt back, then turned toward Barney just as he charged at her.

"Luca." Gabriella shouted.

Kana sprang from the kitchen and bolted toward the front door. Barney missed her by inches.

"Barney," Atlas warned.

"Come back here you stupid, stupid little termagant." He snarled at her for destroying his liquor and raced after her. Barney was going to kill her. Right now. This was his excuse; a shattered bottle of whiskey.

Vincent flew after them, shredding through his clothes in his frantic attempts to stop the Shade from chasing her.

Luca cackled and slapped his thigh. "I love it here."

Kana screamed and hauled the front door open, running with the speed of an antelope with a lion on its tail, with Barney close at her heels.

Vincent had become the giant wolf and barely squeezed his flank through the door as he tore after the pair. He howled a warning but Kana, fuelled by the fear of death. He leapt down the stairs in the garden, vaulted over the small gate, and flew up the dirt path to the road.

Barney thundered after her.

She dared not look back, her breath loud and her heart in her ears.

"Come back here now and I'll make sure it doesn't hurt."

Kana slammed her feet down hoping for more speed.

Vincent leapt, and flattened Barney just as his hand brushed her hair. Kana wobbled, dizziness rushing through her and ran for another few steps under her own momentum before collapsing, her body too exhausted to carry on.

Vincent stood with one bare paw planted on Barney, then sat

heavily upon the hissing, gaunt creature. He barked loud, a soft whine in his tone, but Kana's head spun, she felt dizzy and incredibly weak. She rolled onto her back, and peered through bleary, half lidded eyes.

"Raise up off of me, you oversized lapdog."

"I'm fine," Kana insisted, her heartbeat slowly returning to normal. Her chest hurt.

"Dios mio, Kana." Gabriella's voice felt distant and worried. "Atlas, did he touch her?"

"Not quite. Almost. She sleeps."

"I'm awake," Kana insisted before darkness swept over her.

15

First came awareness, then the realization that her head thumped with her pulse, and Kana's eyes popped open with it. She groaned, and attempted to sit up. Lights flashed behind her eyelids, warning her not to move so fast and she hissed. If she hadn't known better, she'd would swear she was riding through a cataclysm of a hangover.

"Y'aright, Chere?" Chloe's voice was soothing, relaxing and warm and it fluttered around her skull, the tinkling of bells had returned. "You feeling any good?"

Kana opened her mouth and tried to enunciate. All she could manage was a slight whimper.

Chloe chuckled. "You been out for a spell, we were slightly worried, but I gave you some blood to keep you going. You should be fine."

"How.out?" Kana mumbled out the words.

"Try that again?" Chloe giggled, and Kana flopped back onto

the bed.

"How how long?" Her hand reached up to wipe drool from her mouth.

"Couple days. Vincent's been in and out to check on you, Gabriella too. You thirsty?"

Kana nodded slowly, letting her vision settle. Chloe sprawled on her stomach opposite her in a pale blue nightshirt, bare legs tapping her pillow. She held a glass between her hands, filled with blood. A light red mark ringed the glass where the liquid had previously been filled to. It turned her stomach.

"You want a sip?" Chloe tittered, eyeing Kana and noting the slight disgust on her face. "It ain't as bad as my blood."

Kana pulled a face and shook her head. "Don't wanna become a vamp."

Chloe started to laugh again. "It ain't so bad. Besides, takes more than a taste or two. You'd need a ton of vamp blood before you changed. Right now, you're just enhanced a bit. Better than the average human, which ain't nothing bad at all."

Kana turned her eyes to the window. A faint glow of moonlight trickled in. Must be around midnight, judging by the angle of the moon. Not a full moon, but it would be coming soon. It made her wonder what might happen to Vincent.

She watched Chloe holding the glass, "It's it hard to survive?"

"Back before I found Gabriella's safe house, I had to stay up all night to feed. It's so much harder to be sneaky in the day, except out here."

"That must havebeen rough," Kana rubbed her eyes, the rush from Chloe's blood swimming through her veins, slowly settling as long as she didn't move too fast.

"Nah, a lot of the time I used to hide in basements, cellars. One time I holed up in a twenty four hour store, hid in the ventilation for a couple hours. 'Nother time? I even slept at the bottom of this big ol' lake in the middle of nowhere."

"You didn't drown?"

"Chere, I only breathe 'cause it's a habit. It ain't 'cause I have to. I can't drown. Lungs did fill with water, though. Weirdest sensation." Chloe gave Kana a pleasant smile and took a sip of from her glass.

It left a red moustache above her top lip. Like milk, but not white. She opened her mouth to say just that when the door creaked open.

Vincent's shaggy face peering in with a grin.

Kana waved slightly at him and did her best to return the smile. He looked overjoyed to see her awake. "You girls aren't naked in here, are ya? 'Cause I can always wait until ye are naked an' come back."

"Vincent." Chloe snapped, Kana resisted the urge to burst into laughter at the sight of his face poking around the door. The way his head had popped into view was not unlike a dog discovering his owners were hiding from him.

"Get out, you big jerk! What if we was naked? You didn't even knock."

"You're a vampire, love." Vincent grinned, the rest of his large body slinking into the room, revealing he carried a large, heavy duffel that clinked, suggesting bottles. "Do you knock when you sneak into houses for your midnight snack?" The door clicked closed behind him and he ambled over. In the shadows he looked even larger, but Kana could see his eyes. The glowed with a soft light when he looked at her. She realized, for the first time in her life, she could see quite well in the dark. Something she should thank Chloe for, later.

"That's different, they's prey.

"Kana's a human, is she not prey?" Chloe scoffed, a bit of disgust to her tone. "Or wcrc you getting to that bit after you'd had your girly party?"

"Kana is my friend."

"Well then, and friends don't eat friends, right?"

"Bingo."

He grinned wide, white teeth shining as he nodded a scruffy chin at her, "Scooch up, lass. Make room. I've brought prezzies."

He plonked down on the edge of the bed beside Kana, and propped the bag up against the wall, diving in to fetch himself a bottle. Strong teeth popped off the cap; he spat it absently into the bag before he tipped it toward her in salute and took a large swig. "Glad to see you stirring, lass. It's been too quiet without you. Barney and Luca are giving each other the cold shoulder, and all the rest of us, too. Atlas stayed. He keeps muttering about balance and nature n' other godly Titan stuff."

"Really?" Kana sounded more surprised than she intended, lingering effects of the blood in system. "Atlas is worried about me?"

"Well, it's been tense. But at least it's quiet. Am I interrupting some private engagement? If so, can I watch?" He flashed a wicked grin and Chloe scowled at him. Kana tried to look annoyed. The pair turned to one another and giggled, then hung their heads at the failure of their pretense, but kept giggling.

"I'm teasing you, Chloe." Vincent chuckled. "Kana, you want a bottle? Might help with all the blood Chloe's been feeding you. Thin it a bit, eh? Ever tried rum before? I got some in here. Remember, me and Gabriella were talking about it before Yula burnt the kitchen to kingdom come? It's the closest to that good stuff I could find." He pulled out a bottle, cracked open the cap just as he had with his own and held it out to Kana. She stiffened, "No thanks."

"Oh, come on. It's not the first thing I've done to corrupt you." The wolf man shook the bottle. Kana reached out for it. "Ah, now there you go, lass. It's sweet, it's strong, and it'll put hairs on your chest."

"You're not exactly selling the idea," Kana pulled a face at the thought, peering into the neck of the bottle, and sniffing the mingled sweetness of oak, caramel, vanilla, and anise. She took a swig. The slow burn trickled down her throat. She nodded slightly. "That just might, though."

"You can finish it. Sorry Chloe, I'd offer you one but," he nodded at her cup of blood. "Something tells me your clotting red ooze will suffice."

"Bite me, puppy."

Vincent chuckled loudly. Vincent nudged Kana. "Side effect of sobriety, makes 'em all crotchety. We'll not long suffer the malady, though, eh?"

Kana shrugged, excusing herself from answering with a long slow pull from the bottle. That was interesting to know. Werewolves could get drunk but vampires couldn't.

"Any more of that nonsense, Vincent, and I'll force feed you chocolate."

Vincent scowled, but he remained firmly seated, half perched on the end of Chloe's bed. Kana opened her mouth, shocked.

"You mean he can't have chocolate? Just like a real dog?" She exclaimed. "Seriously?"

Chloe doubled over, a trickle of laughter spilling from her lips. Vincent scowled and barked out a "No."

"No, Kana," Chloe managed, struggling to stop laughing. "It won't hurt him none. He just don't like it." Her laughter reached the noiseless stage, her body shaking so hard that not a sound came out.

Vincent's face straightened. He wasn't amused.

Cheeks pinking, Kana hid herself in the rum bottle once more. How was she supposed to know it was a joke? Not a minute ago she had just learned that vampire's couldn't get drunk. For all she knew Vincent could have been allergic to chocolate.

"So, Kana." Vincent attempted to change the subject. "How you feeling? Barney's been on the naughty step for about three days now, and Atlas has threatened Luca he'd call the Warfather down on him. Getting everyone into trouble like that, I might see to it your own parents come back and sort you out for it. No more smoking behind the bike sheds."

"That's not all that can be done behind the bike sheds, 'Ulf,' is it?" Kana grinned. She saw her chance and she took it.

"Little wench." Vincent growled playfully, but his eyes had widened. She saw his throat flicker in a swallow. Kana snorted into her drink. Had bravery increased, no doubt from Chloe's blood once more thick in her veins? She swirled the bottle and Chloe quietly watched the pair. "Chloe said you were worried about me. That you came to visit."

"Oh, aye." Vincent nodded. "Always looking for stray lumps of meat when the wolf week comes upon us."

" Sure, and I'm guessing Chloe has to stop you from humping the furniture too. Or does Gabriella help with that?"

The room grew silent. The vampire's eyes met the wolf's before diverting south. Vincent blinked. The corner of his mouth twitched.

"Don't you start with that, " He replied, sourly, a frown on his face. "I came in to welcome you back to the land of the living, s'all."

" Sorry, that might've been funnier in my head" Kana immediately felt awful. She hadn't intended to hurt him. "Might just be the drink."

Vincent burst into laughter. "Arse." Kana scowled now, letting out a tiny laugh of her own, shaking his hand from her shoulder.

Chloe shifted, drinking more from her glass. She pondered her glass. "Must be strange for you, Chere. I ain't been human for so long. I bet it's strange lookin' at all of us and knowing you ain't got no powers to defend yourself. That's why I was both happy and surprised that you stayed with us."

"Well, whatever the reason," Vincent chuckled on. "You piss off Barney and you do it without exploding the glassware for fun, and that's more than enough reason to keep you."

"Hear, hear. Cheers to that." Chloe nodded and held out her glass. Vincent followed suit and so did Kana.

"To having the lass here," Vincent offered and the three clinked their glasses together.

Kana had to grin in response. It was good to know that her dislike of Barney was shared by others in the house. In fact, it made her feel much in safer the company of the vampire and the werewolf.

Kana's bedroom door creaked open. Gabriella appeared in the doorway, a look of profound exasperation written across her olive face till she saw Kana sitting up. It softened to a tender, half smile.

"It is dark. The moon is up. Go. To. Sleep."

"Gabby," Vincent grinned. "Come join us, will you? We've got drink." He shook a bottle at her.

"Oh, si, I'd love to, Vincent." Gabriella's voice dripped with sarcasm. "Oh, wait. I just remember. I run a hotel, and I need to sleep. I ask one more time. Go to sleep. Or I start upping rent."

"Well, I'm off." Chloe insisted, hurriedly finding her feet. "Kana, you oughta sleep some more. Then get some nutrition in you. The more conventional kind."

Kana looked at Vincent as he stood and frowned. He hesitated and raised a brow. Kana patted the side of the bed in askance, hoping Gabriella wouldn't see.

"Ease up, Gabriella. Gonna stay here till the little lass falls asleep."

Gabriella's eyes narrowed, yet the tiniest hint of amusement lingered in them. "Fine. But keep it down, cabrón." The door clicked lightly behind her.

Kana nodded, Vincent motioned crossing his heart and plonked back down.

"You alright, lass?"

"What is he anyway?"

"Hmm?"

"Well, you're a werewolf, Chloe's a vampire, Yula's a salamander. What would you call Barney?"

"Fairest I can say is a thing you might not know of." Vincent shrugged, and stared at his bottle. "Have you ever heard of a thing called a Tulpa?"

Kana blinked as she took another swig from her bottle, then shook her head as she swallowed it.

"It's" his tongue ran over his upper lip as he searched for the best way to explain it. "It's an idea. I mean Barney, he's nothing but an idea. And Atlas took the idea and squashed him all down into a limited physical beastie. It's not meant to scare you, lass, but he's Death. Literally. He's the concept of death forced into a definite physical being. That's why he's so angry all the time. He's a force of the universe, Kana, he's not meant to be all tiny and caged in flesh. There are some beings he couldn't touch even before, though. Luca being one of them. And he's now rubbing Barney's nose in his condition, just 'cause he thinks it's fun."

Kana blinked. Her brow furrowed, and she almost felt sorry for Barney. But only almost, and only for a moment.

"All I know is, if he touches you, it's game over. You had a lucky break there."

Kana blinked. "You were worried."

"Aye. In truth, I was. I'd miss you. You liven the place up. With your questions, and all."

Kana's cheeks prickled with warmth and a huge smile rose onto her face. Vincent smiled back, the most genuine smile she'd seen from him yet.

"You'd miss me?" She teased. "Why Vincent, you're starting to sound less like a big bad wolf and more like a family pet."

"I'll give you a bloody pet, lass." Vincent growled. "Only I imagine you'd be too weak for the big bad wolf right now."

Kana eyed the bottle in her hands. She hadn't even half drained it, but she popped it down on the floor, and the carrier of bottles with it. Perhaps the blood had affected her more than she realised, perhaps the tiny amount of drink, or maybe both together.

"Actually," she grinned wide, "I'm just curious if dog kisses have a lot of tongue in them."

Vincent bit his lip and leaned towards her, pinning her between the mattress and his locked arms. "I though you wanted me here to help you fall asleep?" Kana leaned closer. She swallowed. "I wasn't lying when I said I wanted you under me again, Kana. But not tonight."

"Coward." Kana said. "Anyway, wearing me out counts toward making me sleepy, doesn't it?"

"Peer pressure," Vincent chuckled at her, "and logic. Now how could a boy resist?"

"Damn right."

He cut her off mid word. His lips locking with hers and she squeaked; half in earnest, half in surprise. She immediately kissed back, pressing herself against him. The curve of her breasts molded against his solid chest as she kept him close, wrapping her hands around his neck to keep his lips locked to hers. Part of her was afraid of what might happen when it ended, what he might say. It might be awkward, it might not, but she would at least enjoy this for what it was worth.

When he pulled away, she stiffened.

"Am going to hell for this." he muttered, shaking his head. "Lass, I'm sorry."

"Don't be. I'm a grown "Lass" not a wee kid." Kana pulled him back again. She pulled him down upon her, the scorching heat from him enough to negate the need for a blanket. "Now show me that big bad wolf. "

16

She couldn't remember the last time she had awakened so refreshed.

Relaxed and calm, her breathing came slow as she came to, her eyes not yet open. She had yet to move, and when she felt the tug of a thick arm pulled her back, she didn't want to. A noise of satisfaction escaped her, echoed by Vincent behind her.

"How are you feeling, lass?" His words rumbled through her and she smiled, nuzzling deeper into the pillow. Everything in the world seemed right.

"Good." She giggled and snuggled down deeper into his arms.

"Just good? Should I be offended?"

"Mmm. Maybe pretty good." She teased, eyes finally opening. She wriggled closer still, entwining her legs around his and letting the warmth bloom around her. Her eyes stung with the early morning light and her hands reached up to rub the sleep from them.

171

The wolf man captured them and ran his own hand up them to her shoulders, but it did not stop her stretching. Her cradled another arm around her waist.

"Maybe we could do better than that, eh?" He chuckled, brushing his lips against her nose. "Because you sounded much more impressed last night,"

"Later," She stifled a giggle and turned, nestled safe against him, her breath bouncing off his chest and returning hot against her. She placed a kiss on his neck.

Nobody could kidnap her from this bliss.

She had known for a few days that she found him attractive, but she hadn't realised that there could be anything major between them until last night. A pang of guilt hit her, wondering what Gabriella might think.

"Will Gabriella be angry, about us?"

"Not about us, but 'cause you are human, lass. It might warrant a good scolding." Vincent sighed and rolled away, stretching his arms up until they cracked. Kana's body felt chilly without him and she pouted. She followed his movement and pressed her head against his chest, prolonging the contact. Her hand curled along his waist.

"She doesn't need to know. Not for a while." Kana insisted. Something told her getting serious would frighten him away quick. If he cared, he'd be back. Simple as that, but she wasn't ready to leave the warmth of his embrace just yet.

"She'll find out, eventually. Can't seem to stay away from ye' for long. She'll know."

"You can't, huh?" Hearing it made her happy. "Does that mean my bed will be a little warmer from now on?"

"You bet it does. To hell with what Gabby thinks."

He grunted and peeled himself from her, though his hand lingered on hers long enough to suggest he didn't want to leave her touch, either. The heat left with him. The urge to kiss him again burned beneath her skin.

"Right, where's my clothes?"

He found his garments, strewn across her floor, and shrugged them on, tossing hers on the bed for her to collect in her own time.

"Stay," Her voice pleaded. She saw him flinch.

"I want to stay, but your blasted mother is at the door."

"What." Kana yelped and scrambled into her clothes, pulling them on with the bedsheets to shield her. "How?"

Vincent nodded at the open window. If Kana listened carefully, she could hear footsteps walking up the garden path. Now dressed, though slightly unkempt, she ran to the window, running her fingers through her wild curly hair. Craning her neck, she saw the unmistakable form of her mother disappear out of view. The sound of the letterbox slamming down confirmed her presence at the door. A large bird crow cawed forlornly on the fence and tilted its head.

"Shit. What does she want now?"

"S'fine, lass." Vincent whispered, slowly climbing out of the window. "Just make yourself presentable. You don't need to worry about me." He grinned and let himself drop.

"You don't have to leave. " Kana narrowed her brows and watched as the wolf man slipped around the back of the house seconds before Karol peered around. Kana jolted her head back, narrowly missing her mother's gaze. "You could have just hid in the bathroom" she muttered to herself.

"Kana." Just as expected, Gabriella's voice called through.

"Second." Kana ran into her bathroom and splashed her face, trying to wash away sleep and towel away the sweat of last night. She ran her fingers through her hair and took a deep breath before creeping through to the living room. A shower would have to wait.

"Hey, mum." She grinned nervously. "To what do I owe the pleasure?"

"Don't even speak to me, Kana." Karol said shaking her head. "I have all your clothes in this bag. We're going to convert your bedroom since you're so keen on staying here and, as I said, I want all your stuff out of my house if you're no longer staying there."

Kana pursed her lips and frowned. It was impossible everything she owned fit in that bag, but in fairness, she'd had plenty of time to go home and fetch her things herself. She just lacked the courage. "Right." Kana fought the lump growing in her throat. "I'll just take it to my room."

Before she could turn, an excited voice burst into the room.

"Mum. Mum. I'm back from France. And guess what! I just saw

Vincent sneak out of Kana's room! I thought we weren't allowed to mix rooms. You said. Also, I tried some weird cheese when I was there."

Kana whirled. There stood Lola, naked save for Vincent's over-sized shirt on her skinny, bird-like, prepubescent frame. Kana's eyes darted to Karol and Gabriella. For a moment she forgot what oxygen was.

Karol's lips tightened into a firm, thin line and the look of disappointment on her face sent paroxysms of guilt through the Kana's stomach. She's seen anger to many times, but never this level of disappointment. She held her arm out for Kana to take the bag and stalked towards the door.

Gabriella must have already known and didn't care for she ran to her daughter and scooped her up tight. "Lola, mi nina." She whispered and the girl giggled.

"Mum. Put me down. I'm fine. It was Calais, not America or somewhere really far away." But Gabriella would not release Lola till she was certain her daughter had truly made it home safe.

"Well, aren't you a sight for sore eyes?"

Kana's stomach lurched again. Luca had found her mother. "Lola, you're not hurt are you?"

"No, mum. I'm fine. It was kinda fun."

Kana darted to the hall once more. Luca had taken her mother's hand and kissed it with artful suavity. The woman froze and pulled a face of confusion before she burst into something Kana hadn't seen in years; laughter.

"I'm sorry, have we met?"

"Luca." Kana insisted. "Don't."

"Ah, you must be Kana's sister." Luca's grin manifested and Kana swore she understood the meaning of a heart palpitation. Her mother's smile widened.

"Oh, no. I'm her mother." Karol giggled, openly flirting with the handsome Trickster. "Though she treats me like something she scraped from her shoe. The trouble she's put me through. Are all children so ungrateful?" She shot Kana a look as she spoke.

"Tsk tsk tsk." Luca shook his head. "Children are so difficult aren't they? You give and you give, and still it is not enough. I have a daughter of my own. She's a pretty little thing, but has such a fierce temper. Girls are so controlling at times. Mine's is a little hell raiser."

"I understand completely." Karol muttered. "I thought I'd raised her right but I guess not. "

"Madam, believe me, I understand. The thought of my own daughter bed hopping with strange men, " he tutted, enjoying his game. "Bad business."

"Yes, I cannot control her stubborn behaviour anymore. She is on her own." Karol turned a strange shade of red and continued towards the door.

Luca however wasn't through causing trouble. He quickly interrupted her stride, side stepping into her path. "Yes. To have one's daughter playing house with such monstrous creatures."Would you care to see just how ghastly things are here? How much danger your daughter is in?"

"What?" Karol recoiled, backing up. "What do you mean, danger? Is that why the police were here?"

Luca waggled his finger and pointed into the living room. Gabriella turned to look, wary as she finally spied the Trickster with Karol.

"Luca, what are you doing?"

But the Trickster snapped his fingers and inside a globule of light flickered Gabriella's image, like a bad analogue television signal. Her form turned into an icy golem with ice daggers for teeth.

Karol stumbled back.

"Take the Ice Queen for example; hardly a suitable replacement for a mother's warmth." Luca tutted again. "Or her daughter, the sneaky little shape shifter who can take any form."

Lola looked up in time for Luca to snap his fingers. Kana almost screamed as a thousand different forms reflected across the twelve year old; a crocodile, a bear, a lion, all in a matter of seconds.

Karol inhaled sharp and stepped back.

Luca curled his hand across her shoulder. "Something wicked, my dear, does not this way come. It's here already."

At that precise moment, Barney himself appeared from the kitchen and growled at the sight the images rippling across Gabriella and Lola.

"Luca, what do you think you are playing at?"

Luca grinned, and Barney too, changed.

Kana's stomach bottomed out as she watched the skin on Barney's face slough off to reveal bloody sinew, yellowing bloodshot eyes. His lipless mouth became a grin of razor sharp rotted teeth, and his bony fingers tapered into scythe-like points. The muscles on his face rippled, wet and glistening.

Karol screamed.

"Enough, Luca." Gabriella shouted. "Enough, stop it. This is beyond a joke now. I will shout for Atlas."

Karol grabbed for Kana and hauled her towards the door. The bag of clothes dropped from Kana's grasp and landed with a heavy thump on the hallway.

"We're leaving." The woman screeched. "Kana, you're coming home. You can't stay here any longer. If I have to drag you every step of the way, I will."

Kana fought with every inch of her strength. "No. I'm not going, I'm safe here. You don't understand. Luca, stop it."

"Good, take the brat."

"Go to hell, Barney." Kana spat at him, she tried to pry loose from her mother's grip. "Get off me, Mother."

"What's going on?" Chloe appeared from the top stair. "Kana, what are --?"

"Ah, the oldest of the fiends, the most well known and feared; the vampire." Luca pointed at Chloe and Kana felt the woman's insistence they leave renewed as the image of Chloe opened her mouth to hiss, showing needle teeth and pallid skin, and slits for eyes. It sent shivers down Kana's own spine.

"No, Luca, stop. Mum, you don't understand. That's not real, Luca is tricking you. That's what he does. It's an illusion. Let me go."

"Kana, you are insane. We are going to the police. We can't have people like this running around, threatening our safety."

"Mum, for once just listen to me."

"Stop this at once." Gabriella interrupted, storming over to Luca, but as Karol finally pulled Kana out of the front door, a loud pop echoed through the house. Luca reappeared in the garden, sitting merrily enough on the hotel sign. The paint had been altered to form the words "Well Done".

"So many horrible beasties to eat your daughter, suck her blood and poison her mind against you; how devilishly clever of them."

"Luca.." The wolf man bounded over, shirtless and every inch of him covered in hair. He needed no illusion. Teeth were razor sharp, his muzzle half grown, his claws scraped the fence as Vincent stood to bar Karol's path.

"The varulv,I believe you call him werewolf." Luca laughed aloud with glee. "How ferocious in form; how base and bestial in his appetites."

"That's not what you told Mother when I was born." Vincent almost grinned as he snarled the words.It did nothing to soften his look to Karol, whose grip on Kana tightened.

"Of course it was. The mortal thinks these are warnings,they are boasts."

Gabriella held her head in both her hands. "Dios mio, there goes the neighbourhood."

"Vincent," Kana whined. "Vincent? Kana, that thing was in your bedroom?"

"No. Mum. You don't understand anything that's going on. If you'll let me just explain-"

"Oh I understand plenty. You are a stupid girl. You're not safe here., I'm taking you home before you get yourself killed. I should have paid more attention. I should have seen the danger. We're going straight to the police."

"Oh no, you're not." Vincent growled.

Luca chuckled. "No-one will believe a word." His chuckle grew into guffaws. "Enjoy your one-way ticket to Crazy Town, though."

Lola had been trying to barge past her mother who stood in the front door. She finally escaped into he front garden in the form of a brown rat, and reformed as a girl. Naked as a babe, she shouted at Kana's mother.

"No. You are not taking Kana back." She stomped her foot. "She's family. She's staying here where she belongs. She's my new sister."

Gabriella pulled her daughter back and wrapping her in the shirt that had dropped.

"Aye, lass. You tell her." Vincent blocked their path. "She belongs here. With us and with me"

Amidst the chaos, Luca laughed, and laughed.

Kana heard a strange thump from above as a window slid open and both Yula and Atlas poked their heads out of a large upstairs window.

"Kana. I heard shouting." Yula sounded startled. "What's happening?"

"She's coming home with her mother." Karol yelled back.

Luca did not bother showing Karol the Salamander's form. Indeed he appeared far too busy trying to avoid falling from the sign in his amusement of the trouble he had caused as he rocked dangerously back and forth.

Barney barged into the garden too. Karol backed up from him, closer to Vincent and the gate. She seemed to regret her decision when the wolf man growled.

"What are you doing, Yula?" Barney shouted up, seeing her in the same room with Atlas, something that clearly was not supposed to happen.

"She is allowing me to bind her fire, Barnabus." The Titan sternly defined. "We discussed it and it is for the best."

"Tell me you are not doing this willingly."

"I said I would, BarneyI don't want hurt anyone. Gabriella promised me a fireplace, a heater, and a good home." "This is preposterous." The Shade snarled, flinging one hand toward Kana, "The little witch is being carted off. There's no need now."

Looking through the open window, Yula shook her red head. "I must be bound, I can't let anything else happen, I'm sorry. I love you Barney, but I can't." The tiny salamander whimpered and sniffled. "Don't you dare, Yula." Barney growled. " I forbid it."

"I can, and I will, Barney. I'm sorry."

"No. I won't allow it." The tulpa roared, his voice echoing across the empty fields. Kana backed up against her mother's side.

Yula drew in a breath and began to bubble into tears.

"Barney," Gabriella warned. "Stop it now. Don't upset her. Remember last time. Please. She could destroy my house."

He was raging, beyond reason. "Do you only think of yourself? I cannot have this. You are being selfish, Atlas. What is she to me with her spark?"

"Barnabus, enough discussion." The grandfatherly Titan gave a frown. "We are going through with this. You will obey me."

"No."

"Maybe Barney is right." Yula turned into full blown tears at hearing he only needed her for her gift of fire. Sobbing like a woman with a broken heart, she retreated from the window.

"Damn right I am. Don't you dare fight me on this, Yula." Barney stormed back into the house with Gabriella running at his heels.

Lola backed up and returned her attention to Kana. "You can't let your mum take you. You're part of this family now." She whimpered, tears brimming in her beautiful purple eyes. The girl wrapped her arms around Kana's waist and clung tight, sobbing.

For the first time, Karol relinquished her grip on her daughter and a look of pity crossed her face.

A crack like a gunshot sent all eyes skyward.

Karol and Kana both squealed as the entire window that was once occupied by Yula and Atlas burst outward in a glittering cloud of broken glass. Vincent howled and grabbed his child, his woman and her mother, yanking them through the gate. The shower of glass covered the front garden, but did not hit them.

By some miracle Luca remained uninjured.

"Shit, Kana. Get into your mother's car," Vincent snarled, ushering them towards it. "Now, Lola," he yelled at his daughter. "I mean it."

Karol –had already pushed Lola and Kana towards the Volvo, glad to finally have the gate free. The three climbed into the car as Vincent turned and ran, disappearing into the building.

Luca popped again and disappeared.

They waited.

Kana refused to close her door. She wouldn't leave without a fight. Monsters or not these people were her family, her friends, they had kidnapped her, but she loved them. She couldn't just leave them.

"Please let everything be okay," She whimpered. She could still hear shouting, but the voices all merged together, overpowered by the bellow of Barney's furious roaring.

Lola pressed her nose to the window in the back seat and let out a whine. Karol stared half gaping.

A red light flashed behind the broken window.

Kana drew in breath. "No."

It happened in less than a tenth of a second. An almighty explosion rocked Kana's world. The blast wave coming from the house struck the car hard enough to send it skidding sideways, up onto two wheels. The moment felt like an eternity. She saw a column of flame go up into the sky, followed by a cloud of ash.

Her body lurched. With her seatbelt unbuckled and the door open, the blast channelled through the car. It pushed the tilted vehicle like a giant hand, throwing Kana against the windscreen and pushed her body through it. Her head crashed against the ground, hitting only dirt. Glass stung her skin.

Everything went numb.

She heard a scream, a caw, and watched a crow fly out of the back window of the car.

Then came sheer darkness.

***

Her eyes flickered, opened. Flashes of light swam across her blurred vision. Nothing resembled a shape, but enough to pick out vague colours.

"Oh Kana, I am so sorry, Chere."

A flash of blonde flickered by her face and something wet hit her lips. Kana groaned and stirred, peering blankly. Her tongue poked out to touch the wetness and recoiled, tasting something acrid yet so familiar. Everything hurt. Sleeping hadn't hurt, and fighting the tired waves rolling through her aching body seemed like such a stupid, pointless idea. Her head and stomach roiled, and the sensation of noise echoed behind her eyes, as though it boomed from inside her skull.

A zip noise echoed passed her ears, followed by the fumble of paper so loud it could have been ten thousand sheets scrunching in tandem, and finally the beep of buttons like a siren.

"Hello? Is this emergency services? I need to report a bomb. Yes, the little inn. There was a car, two people severely injured. No, the inn is gone. No survivors there."

The voice hitched, wobbled and the pitch peaked.

"Please, send an ambulance, send the police. Hell, send everything. Help."

Her eyes fought to stay open but vision refused to process.

"Kana, stay with me, Chere. Please, stay with me, please. I can't lose you too. Kana. Please." The sensation of arms engulfed her. The icy cold touch numbed the pain, if only slightly. "I won't leave till they come."

But Kana eyes were too heavy. She surrendered to sleep.

17

The rising keen of brakes alerted Kana and Theo to the slowing of the train and the upcoming stop. Several passengers around them tugged their belongings together as they prepared to disembark. Kana hoisted Michael up before pausing, realising that her male companion did not appear to be coming with her.

She hurried to finish her story before they arrived at her stop. She had started and there was no way she could bear to leave without telling him the end.

"The hospital held us for about three weeks." Kana explained, absent-mindedly stuffing the man's canteen into her holdall and scooping Michael up as she stood. "When we went home, there were police. We came up with a story they would believe. Everyone decided it was a gas leak, in the end. It levelled the whole house. Everything was gone"Do you think anyone survived?"Theo rose to his feet after her, his expression speaking of sympathy. "Anyone at all?"

" I think Chloe did. I swear I heard her voice. It had to be hers. Without her blood, there was no way I would have survived. Without her, I wouldn't have had Michael." She kissed the squirming lump in her arms.

He whined and nuzzled his mother, blue eyes peering at Theo with the tiniest squint. "I found out about him three months afterward. I love him. He is all I have left." "I completely understand." Theo smiled and reached out towards him. "He has your eyes." Michael squirmed but did not pull away. Kana let him stroke Michael's cheek with the back of his hand. "Do you think Vincent survived, then?"

"I don't know if anyone did. I mean, if Atlas was killed in the blast, Barney would have been free. If that happened, I guess Gabriella would have died too. I just can't bear to think about it."

"Well, that is some story." Theo seemed genuinely impressed. Kana nodded solemnly and pulled her luggage to her shoulder. The train staggered to a complete stop, brakes screeching even louder.

"You left this part out of your story, though."

"Mm?" Kana slung her pack over the arm not holding the child.

"This part. You haven't explained why you're on the train. I'm curious. How about how 'there' got you to here."

"Oh, you're right." Kana rested Michael on her hip and began to rummage through her bag again. She rustled through papers and pulled out a red envelope. Sifting through the contents, she pulled out a small, badly misspelled letter and handed it to Theo.

"I got this letter several weeks ago. In it were train tickets, plane tickets, and about eight hundred pounds in cash. And a note. Take a look."

Theo did. He unfolded the letter and quickly scanned the words on the page:

Dear Kana,

I figure that the events leading up to the destruction of Gabriella's hotel have been powerful overwhelming. I think many of us still got healing to do. we lost a lot, all of us and that includes you. I understand if you lost your taste for living with us.

If that's how it is, we put a little money together for you to help you out. It was actually Lola's idea. she misses you.

we come all the way to china. I never been before, but we're out in the boonies. Reminds me of back home in Louisiana, I about fell over from surprise. It's easier to move around without worrying about identification. We -- I -- hope very much you decide to come find us. Our home is your home, darlin. We're a weird family, may-be a scary family, but we're your family in our hearts. That's what the tickets are for. If you decide to come home again, we all hope you will -- they will take you home to us. Sorry bout not putting the address on here but you know how things are for us right now. Just follow the ticket trail and you should find us easy enough.

    I don't think any of us will ever forget you. I know Gabriella thought of you like her own daughter.

    much love,
    chloe.

Theo's eyes crinkled, showed a little dampness at the corners, and he handed the letter back. Kana offered him a tender smile and quickly stuffed it back into the envelope.

"I used a lot of the money buying food, and traveling between the ticket destinations. Chloe did her homework on the big stations, but not so much on the others, so I've been making do."

"What if the house isn't there?" Theo interrupted, just as she headed to the carriage door. Kana shushed him. "I'm not meant to think about that. I really can't. I've come this far; I have to keep going."

Theo nodded and pulled the girl into an impromptu hug. Kana recoiled, startled at first, but softened when she realised he intended no ill will. The whistle blew outside, signalling the train intended to move on.

"Good luck, then." He offered. " I hope you find the place."

"Yeah. I'll find it. I have to." Kana almost fled to the door. "I have to go. Thank you. Thank you so much for letting me talk about it. And thank you for the food."

"My pleasure. "

"I have to go. Thank you again."

Kana slipped from the train down onto the platform.

Theo watched through the tiny window as she turned towards the crowd and rummaged for her next set of tickets, clutching the babe tightly to her hip. Her head swung left and right before she disappeared, darting off towards the exits. Theo grinned and leaned forward, his fingers bridging. Having reached the busiest and second last stop, the carriage remained almost deserted. Not a single person entered the train.

"I do hope she finds the place alright." He muttered to himself, smirking wide, "Can't imagine having my Grandchild in any harm's way. That simply would not do."

With a glance upwards, he tilted his head.

The still flickered light bulb above him flared in a sourceless sunlight until it shone whole again. He gave a slight grin, and settled back down into the carriage.

18

Kana wiped the sweat from her forehead and pushed dark brown curls away from her face. The heat hurt. Michael whimpered in her arms, cuddling tight. She panted out encouragement, both for him and herself. "Come on, baby. Nearly there." In truth, Kana had no idea if that was true or not. It felt as though she had walked the world over.

Flies and mosquitoes chewed her sticky bare arms, Michael's too, and no doubt the heat alongside them caused the discomfort of the small child. She'd brought him this far, there was nothing else to do but keep going.

Is it madness, stubborn stupidity, or sheer willpower forcing me on?

But she did not stop to consider the options. If she stopped, she would not start moving again. It physically hurt to imagine how Michael felt. Her fingers tightened around him as she plunged bodily through thick trees, tangled roots and vicious undergrowth that threatened to trip her with any miscalculated step.

Her throat burned with thirst. The empty canteen was useless now; Michael drank the last of the soup six hours ago, and there was nothing for miles. There was only the call of animals; of birds, and insects and the snap of plants underfoot.

If she still headed North, there was hope. There was nothing else but hope, now; but she had to press on. Step by step she trudged, pulling her legs up like a draught horse to carry her own weight, her child, and the luggage around her shoulder that had dug in enough there was a red mark along the flesh.

Michael's wailing echoed out too but Kana had nothing more to give him. She had brought him into this mess. "I'm. Sorry. Baby." She could only pant before exhaustion shuddered her body with a yawn so wide her jaw popped painfully. She winced. She walked on. "We're so close. You'll get to meet your big sister Lola and Aunt Chloe."

She couldn't even be sure who the reassurance was meant for now, her or the child, but she walked forward in the tempo of her words. Her heartbeat beat rapid in her chest despite the slow unsteady gait she picked across the thick mass of plants and leaf litter.

"Lola," she continued, her voice nothing but a croak, "will play so many games with you. Maybe turn into something scary, but she is a good girl. She will never hurt you, baby. And Chloe seems scary, but she is the sweetest vampire you'll ever meet." She croaked laughter as the surreality of the statement struck her. Her foot wobbled as she placed it, the muscles giving way but she snarled, righted her centre of gravity and persisted.

"And Michael my love; your Daddy is a very hairy man, but he's very loving with those he lets into his heart. I think he will love you, so much" A mosquito landed on Kana's arm. It tickled its path up to her elbow and Kana's vision landed on it as the proboscis uncurled and searched for blood supply. Stick shambling forward, Kana reached to slap it, missed, but the insect droned and zipped off. So many bugs.

Salty sweat rolled in fat beads down Kana's face and she let out a sob. Her own mother knew she was missing by now, but they would never track her out here. Even if they pinpointed her location in China, the jungles were too dense, the landmass too large for one tiny human being and her young child.

She would die here.

No.

The fight was not gone completely from her. So long as she drew breath, no matter how much it hurt or burned, ached or nipped, stung or prickled, Kana would find them. This was more than just a retreat, more than just an escape. It was home.

Kana stumbled over a tree root and ran to catch herself. Knotted brown hair tangled further as she twisted and slammed her left side into a sloping tree trunk. Michael narrowly missed it, and she grunted as the slam ricocheted up her arm. She hoped the pain would invigorate some primal urge to keep going, but nothing happened. Her adrenaline remained depleted.

Another mosquito found her arm and she lacked the motivation to swat this one. It broke the skin and sucked. Kana felt the nip, if only in the back of her mind. A new pain, strong enough to remind her of her lucidity. There would be no waking from this dream; either she found the new house, or she died of exhaustion here. Michael would follow soon after, helpless and weak in an inhospitable environment.

The thought broke her heart, but her body lacked the hydration to form tears. That explained the burning headache pulsating through her.

"Now, you won't let me drink from you, but you'll let that creature?" Chloe's voice chastised her in her own mind. Kana staggered blindly, laughing silently at that scolding. The salt of her sweat stung her eyes, blurring her vision. Her arm almost rose to wipe it, the ground disappeared from under her and she fell.

Trees scraped her arms and side and she had no energy to push a scream through her throat as she tumbled. Any last remaining energy she had, she used to keep Michael tightly cradled, her body curled so as not to squash him beneath her. Her spine smacked a tree, slowing her descent and fresh pain seared up her spine. The holdall strap snapped and it raced further ahead, propelled by it's own weight.

"Well, fuck." She croaked, and coughed out something of a laugh. After all this time, still these things had to happen.

Peering down, she watched Michael peer quizzically up at her for just a moment, as if asking, "What the hell are you doing?" before he wailed frantically. Safe in her arms, he remained uninjured. She pulled him tighter to her chest, relieved.

It took a few minutes to pull herself up from the ground but Kana forced her way up and onto her feet again for Michael's sake. Up, she used the tree as support, waves of pain emanating up and down her spine; then she slowly scuffed her way down the rest of the sharp hill. The bag lay at the bottom, less to carry, and her shoulders flexed, free of the weight.

"So close." She reminded the wailing Michael, and herself, and stepped forward. Inch by inch. "I promise, we'll get there. We will. We will."

She watched the ground, measuring the steps between her and the bag. Five. Four. Three The ground flattened off and Kana almost wept as the clearing faded into hazy view.

A mirage. It could only be a mirage.

Her bottom lip wobbled to fight the rising panic in her exhausted body. She dry retched and fumbled for the strap, her eyes never leaving the brick house in the centre of the wooded clearing. It couldn't be real, she decided, it looked too obvious, too out of place.

She dragged the holdall, tugged the strap and whispered, "It's there, baby. It's there. We're home. I promise. We're home." She whimpered. "We're home,"

The word stuck on loop, she repeated them till she sank to her knees at the front door. The door pushed open with her weight and slammed against the hallway wall.

"What the hell? Kana."

Kana smiled, sobbed, and peered up at a flash of blonde.

"You came, Chere?"

Kana found the ability to nod.

"Kana. You came home." Lola bounded at her from out of nowhere, then stopped. "Oh, hey. Where'd you get a baby?"

"Michael. His name is Michael."

"Oh my." Chloe giggled weakly. "Won't that be a lovely surprise?"

"Is is " Kana bit her tongue hard. She couldn't sleep yet. She had to know. "Is he here?"

Chloe gave her a smile, laughed nervously, and wiped her eyes. Lola called out his name.

Out the corner of Kana's eyes, she saw Vincent run to her. In seconds, he scooped her from the threshold and tugged her up, child and all. His heat scorched her, but she held tight and mewled within his arms.

"Vincent, this is Michael." She managed and her heart fluttered at the proud affectionate look on his face.

"He's beautiful, Kana."

She smiled. It was the kind of smile that holds exhaustion and happiness and nervousness all together in a beautiful thing, and before she said her next words, she could see in his eyes that he already suspected. "This is our son."

19

"I can't believe you made it all the way out here." Chloe shook her head in amazement. "To make it so far on your own, and with a baby." She sat beside Kana at the kitchen table; Vincent sat to her right, nursing a drink of something clearly alcoholic.

"Well, it wasn't exactly easy." Kana said, watching Lola play with Michael on the kitchen floor. She slumped down into one of the wooden kitchen chairs. "The tickets you sent helped, though. The money too. I almost didn't think I was going to make it."

"I knew you would." Vincent nodded sagely. His arms folded and he had a proud grin on his face as he watched the two play. Kana liked that grin. Even if Gabriella would not allow Vincent to stake his claim as Lola's father, Kana would not take that from him with regards to Michael. She turned to him and leaned across the kitchen table.

"Why did none of you think to help me, though? Why did none

of you come and collect me when you left?"

"We wanted to, darlin'." Chloe admitted. "You have no idea how nervous we was, though, and the police came along, ambulances, damn near everything came around. For own safety, we had to get out of there while the gettin' was good."

"Si. There was no time to gather everyone and we could not take you and leave your mother." Gabriella waltzed into the kitchen. Kana rose to her feet and ran forward to hug her in reflex. Just as she reached the door however she paused. She could not quite remember the last time she had hugged her real mother nor the last time she wanted to, but just knowing that Gabriella was alive brought a prickle of tears to her eyes and swell of joy in her heart. Just like Vincent's had. While Gabriella had given her more attention than her mother had; all the same, she did not yet know whether the ice queen would accept a hug or not.

"Hi." Kana mumbled and looked at the floor. Gabriella smiled and a breath of amusement escaped her. She reached out and stroked Kana's head. "We missed you, Kana. It was not the same without you around." Gabriella grinned down at her.

"Aye." Vincent nodded but neither he nor Chloe were looking in her direction.

"Can I stay with you again, Gabriella?" Kana asked quietly.

Gabriella's smile only widened at her words.

"As if you even need to ask. Of course you can, mi hija." Gabriella chuckled and brushed past Kana. Her hand squeezed her shoulder as she did so and Kana could help but imagine it felt warm. "Would you like a hot chocolate, Kana?"

Kana faltered for a second, turning as Gabriella flicked open the fridge.

"So, what happened? Why China?"

"Out here people struggle to survive. The jungles are thick. Food is scarce. So we will not be found unless we wish to be." Gabriella explained, and proceed to prepare a mug. "Atlas has left us but he helped us set up a small farm. Food will not be difficult for us."

"Not you, anyway, Gabriella." Chloe said. "You've been around for centuries. You pretty nearly invented farming."

"Not quite." Gabriella said with a nod. "But there are no goats."

Kana raised a brow at Vincent who narrowed his eyebrows in return.

"How did you all make it out of there alive?" Kana asked again. "The blast hit the car so hard it went skidding sideways. I thought something " Her words faded out. What she had thought didn't need to be said as it was evident enough. Vincent grimaced and sighed. Chloe looked at her feet. Gabriella stopped completely.

"Kana, I need to explain something." Gabriella said bridging her fingers. She looked the young woman in the eye and spoke delicately. "We didn't all make it out. Yula didn't. The blast that rocked the house tore her apart. She burst completely into flame and that was it. She was gone."

Kana's breath stuck in her throat. She swallowed hard. Twice, she tried to form words but nothing more than half syllables stuttered out of her throat.

"I'm sorry." Kana tried.

"Don't be silly, lass. It's not your fault." Vincent growled. Gabriella shushed him.

"It was no-one's fault, Vincent. It happened and we have dealt with the fallout. Kana is here. Yula is not. That's the end of it."

"How is Barney?" The lump in Kana's throat refused to budge and mentioning the tulpa's name only added nausea to that lump. "How is he taking that?"

Gabriella gave a long sigh that shook her entire body. "Not well." She said finally. "Just don't talk to him. Avoid him if you can. Por favor?"

Kana nodded. She would try her best.

The hot chocolate seemingly forgotten, Gabriella stared into the cupboard. The hot chocolate stared back but the woman's mind was elsewhere. Kana backed up.

"I'm going to go find another room to settle into." Kana said uneasily and turned towards the stairs. A part of her wondered how they had created such a similar house to the first so quickly. Perhaps Atlas had helped out. It wouldn't surprise her if one of the house mates had a power for such things. She headed up slowly. Her legs still burned from the long trek through the jungle and she longed to bathe and rest but she wouldn't leave Michael for too long.

A whining mumble disturbed her search and she turned to follow it on tiptoe. She stopped cold. Gabriella had literally told her moments ago to stay away from Barney, and there he was. She peered in through the half open door and saw him lying there whimpering like a distrought child.

Was he crying? Her eyebrows rose and her jaw dropped to the floor.

"Come to gloat, mortal?" He did not turn to face her but his deep baritone voice rumbled out around the room, it was laced with tears. "No." She said firmly. "I wouldn't dream of it."

He still didn't look up. After a moment, she took a few steps forward towards the curled up leather clad bundle on the bed. She heard a sniffle and laid a hand on his shoulder, being careful not to touch his skin.

"You're a freak." he said quietly.

"Yeah, I am." she replied. "Completely unnatural. I'm sorry."

"It should have been you."

"I know."

"Get out." He said.

Kana nodded and backed up. She wiped her eyes. Already she could feel tears dripping down her cheek and she resisted a sniff of her own.

"Do you want to know why I came back?" Kana asked.

No reply.

"I came back because despite everything, you lot are the closest to family I've ever felt. Even though you hate me, Barney, you've stuck around too. Gabriella's kind of like a mother to me. She's been good to me. I guess in a way you're a better father than I've ever had. Or maybe you'd suit the sulky older brother type. If you wanted, I-."

"Stop." Barney said. His voice raised barely above a whisper. "I don't want to hear it. Go away."

"My point," Kana continued. "is that, despite everything, you have been more emotionally available to me than any blood family I have. I don't care if you think you're all monsters or that I can't be here because I'm not, or that I'm on a different scale of monster. This is my home. Like it or not, you are my family now."

"Kana." Barney sat up. He hunched over the opposite side of the bed and pressed his palms to his eyes. "If I tell you I appreciate the sentiment, will you leave? I do not care to hear it. Yula is gone and it is my fault."

"It's not your fault."

"It is." Barney snarled. "She threatened to take out the entire town in a blazing inferno and I have to take her lest she kill absolutely everyone. You know nothing. To feel the same thoughts, the same pain, the same horror that those you kill feel when you take them? You understand nothing. Now get out."

A wave of sympathy passed through Kana that she could not control and she stood her ground.

"I'm still sorry."

"I don't care."

"Well, I am sorry, so there." Kana turned on her heel. She had no reason to stick around to be rebuffed. He needed his space and she would give it to him. He had confided in her and that, at least, was progress. "I hope you feel better, Barney. When you get a moment, my son is downstairs. You should come down and see him."

"Lovely, more humans in the house." Barney growled, sounding more like himself now, less like a beaten soul.

"Of course, except he isn't all human. He is Vincent's son" Kana tried not to grin at being able to finally say those words aloud. Leaving him alone with those thoughts, she headed out the door and up the corridor, searching for an empty room.

"How precious."

A voice made Kana spin.

In the corner of the hallway stood Luca.

Kana glared at him. After the stunt he pulled in the garden of the old house, she didn't entirely know how to take him. She folded her arms and the grin on his face multiplied tenfold. "Well. You made it here and in one piece. I am both impressed and surprised. The wolf pup made it too."

"Luca." Kana said, keeping her distance. "What do you want? Are you still living here?"

"Naturally. I love it here. So. Much. Fun. But you know, I don't think this one should be blown up. Not with such a cute little child running around. What do you think?" He leaned towards her with his eyes widened like saucers. "Illusions? Lycanthropy? Regeneration? What will the little one have I wonder?"

"Why would he have illusions?" Kana squinted. "That's your power."

"Yes. It is." Luca cackled with glee. "But wouldn't it be amusing?Let's pretend for one moment, that the child was mine. What power should he have?"

"He's not yours." Kana didn't like this. "Not even a little bit."

"Oh, darling. Of course he is my precious family. You should ask Ulf about that." He finished with a flourish, waving his hand and disappeared.

Kana bolted downstairs.

"Vincent." She shouted. "Lass. What?" The werewolf's voice echoed out into the hall. Kana reached the kitchen door and shot him a panicked look.

"Luca says Michael is his family. What does that even mean? How could that be? He's yours."

Vincent faltered and stood. Like a kicked puppy he stared at the ground. His actions only caused Kana greater unease.

"Vincent?" She pressed.

Vincent took a deep breath.

"Luca is my father."

Lightning Source UK Ltd.
Milton Keynes UK
UKOW04n1059260716

279215UK00006BA/68/P